LEGENDS OF DREEGAHNNA

Volume 1

S. Marcum

GoToPublish LLC
1-888-337-1724
www.gotopublish.com
info@gotopublish.com

CONTENTS

CHAPTER ONE

It was a dark and dreary night. A fare rain fell in a steady tempo, drumming on the leaves of every tree. The forest of Dartmoor stood silently as the rain fell on its branches. The rain created a light fog which rolled lazily through the trees, mingling in the leaves, and settling amongst the ancient roots of a great forest; it gave the forest an eerie, almost other worldly feel. Save for the croaks of frogs, it was quiet. The silhouette of a figure slowly emerged from the fog.

A tattered brown cloak with a hood rested on his shoulders and head, giving him meager protection against the steady rain. As he walked, his leather boots slowly sunk into the muddy road, making a sloshing sound with every step he took. The figure paused as he saw a light in the distance, like that of a light house beckoning a ship at sea to safe harbor. The figure moved closer to the light; revealing the silhouette of a building. A sign hung by a wooden door with iron fittings. The sign read "Dim Lantern Tavern & Inn" A couple horses stood in a stall made of moss-covered stone and wood.

The figure stood before the building and could hear laughter and merriment inside. He opened the door to find men sitting at tables drinking tankards of ale and grog. A thin balding man with a mustache stood behind a bar on the left of the door. He had sweat to his brow as if he had been working hard all evening to maintain the happiness of the patrons. The man looked at the figure as he wiped soap and water from a tankard and said "Welcome to the Dim Lantern." The figure walked over to the bar and lowered their hood; revealing a young man in his early twenties. He had a small amount of hair on his chin and under his nose. His hair was kept in a pony tail at shoulder length, and dirt covered his cheeks, as if he had been working in a mine for hours.

The young man approached the bar and looked to the bartender. "Sir...." he said with a shiver in his voice. "I am in need of directions." The bartender finished cleaning the tankard he had in his hand and placed it on the bar. He then looked at the young man while drying his hands on his apron.

"And where are you trying to go lad?" said the bartender in a deep Scottish accent.

"I need to get to the other realm." A silence fell on the tavern and most of the patrons within ear shot turned and looked at the young man.

The bartender leaned onto the bar and whispered sternly, "Lad you don't want to go there. We humans are not welcome by the creatures of yor."

The young man had a timid look to him. He shook his head and replied pleadingly, "But I have to get there! Someone important has been taken from me by a troll. Please sir anything you can tell me will help." The bartender let out a sigh and rubbed his temple.

"Lad, I can tell that yur a shy thing. One like you would not fare well in that place, and if I tell ya how to go there, and ya get hurt...." The bartender let out a small huff "Who was taken from ye?"

The young man gave the bartender a hard, determined look, took a deep breath, and spoke again, keeping his voice low but with more control, "My sister. She's the only family I have after our father was taken by sickness. Our mother died during child birth. Please sir I don't have much but I can pay." The young man retrieved a small sack from his belt and poured it onto the bar. A few gold, silver, and copper coins spilled out. The bartender sifted his finger through the pile and looked through his brow at the young man.

"Fine lad, but your death will not be on me. Follow the setting sun into the forest for three days. Then ye should find a clearing with a large rock surrounded by a small meadow. That is your destination; I wish I knew how to open the gate, but I fear only the fairy folk can do that. Ya can stay here for the night in the barn loft. We have no other rooms vacant for now. I'll see ya off in the morning with a morsel of bread for your journey."

The young man looked immediately relieved, and with a short bow replied a quick "Thank you, sir" to the bartender. He then stepped outside and looked to the barn adjacent to the tavern. The barn was typical for the land. Stone base and wooden supports at its corners. A weather-beaten wooden roof gave cover to the barn. The smell of straw, hay, and horse dung filled his nose as he entered. An old ladder sat leaning on the loft to his left. The young man climbed the ladder and rolled onto a pile of straw. He stared at the wooden roof and thought of his sister and her safety. How far will he need to go? Was she still alive? As the thoughts of her raced through his head, he soon fell asleep and dreamed of a time when things were simple. A time before his sister was taken and they lived on their small farm. Him tilling the field with ox and plow and her milking their only goat.

It may not sound like much, but it was his life, his family, normality. *"Sam! We are almost out of bread!" His sister shouted from the doorway of their small stone and straw house. "You will have to take some firewood to market and use the coin for a loaf." Sam shouted back to her as he picked rocks from the freshly tilled field and threw them to the side in a pile. "Could you come with me to market? The baker always raises the price when he sees me." "Emily I must finish tilling the field. I have to plant the crops if we are to survive this winter. Go to market and sell the wood; I shall have a talk with the baker when I see him next. And take your dagger as well. The sheriff stopped by yesterday and told me to be on watch for highwaymen." Emily huffed at her brother and took a shawl from the house and wrapped her shoulders in it. She grabbed a large wicker basket and filled it with cut logs. Taking a strap that was on the basket and placing it on her back she began walking down the old dirt road to the nearby town of Tavistock.*

Samuel took a small rag and dipped it in a wooden bucket of water then wiped his brow. As the day started to end a few hours later, Emily had not yet returned. Samuel became worried for her safety, as the night was a time of darkness and creatures not of the mortal world walked the earth. He grabbed his cloak and a small short sword and began to walk the road. He walked for miles and still saw no sign of her. He soon found himself at Smithville; The gates of wood and walls of logs sharpened at end gave a feeling of protection.

"Lad! Hey lad! Ye awake up there?" Samuel opened his eyes and rolled over to the edge of the loft. The bartender was standing on the ground looking up at him as the morning sun poured in behind him through the open barn door. "Yes sir. I shall be down in a moment." Samuel yawned wiping the sleep from his eyes. After climbing down the ladder, the bartender handed Samuel a small cloth with a morsel of bread and cheese. "Here lad." Samuel took the small package and looked to the bartender.

"Thank you, sir, for your kindness." The bartender breathed a heavy sigh through his nose. "Lad, I know she's your last bit of family, but the creatures of old do not take kindly to human kind. She may already be gone, boy." Samuel tucked the food in his shirt as the bartender spoke. "I know sir. But I have to try. I need to know if she is gone." The bartender looked down and reached in his pocket; pulling a gold coin from it. "Here lad. Take this coin and keep it on ye. The rider of death fears gold." Samuel took the coin and looked strangely at the bartender. Samuel stepped out of the barn and looked to the forest across the way. A foreboding mist sat close to the ground and rays of light darted through gaps in the tree tops. Samuel took a breath and walked over to the forest edge. He sat down at the forest edge and took out the bread and cheese; taking only small bites. For he did not know how long he would be gone and this was his only food.

As he chewed his food, he sat and thought back to his dream. More of a nightmare than memory. He thought back to him standing at the village gates of Tavistock. How the wooden fortifications offered protection.

Samuel opened the gate and found a scene of carnage. A few of the buildings were on fire and a cart sat in the middle of the street where bodies were being stacked by two men. The sheriff stood next to the cart with his hand on the hilt of his sword. The sheriff turned and looked at Samuel and motioned for him to come. Samuel walked over to the sheriff with a heaviness in his heart. Was his sister one of the bodies in the cart, he thought. "Young Samuel. The village was attacked by a troll." The sheriff said as he put his hand on Samuel's shoulder.

"I know it sounds as the raving of a lunatic, but it is true. I saw it with my own eyes. Your sister was taken with a few others by the creature. I'm sorry lad. She's gone." Samuel looked to the ground as a fear built in him. His only family was now gone. Taken to be eaten by a creature in another realm. "Sir. How can I find the realm of creatures?" The sheriff was taken back by Samuel's question. "Samuel. I promised your mother I'd look after you. I will not let you end your bloodline in a foolish manner." "Sir is not my bloodline mine to do as I please? I need to save Emily if at all possible. Please." The sheriff stood and looked at Samuel. "Alright. You are a young man now. There is a tavern south of here on the main road. It is a halfway point between here and Plymouth. It is called the Dim Lantern. The bartender there has the information you seek, but it will come at a price and he may not tell you." Samuel thanked the sheriff and began to walk away. His hand gripping his sword handle. "Samuel! Watch for highwaymen on your journey." Samuel nodded and was off.

A days walk later and the last bit of Samuel's money gone. He now sits on the edge of a forest filled with a motive of heroism or revenge. After sitting all day, the sun soon started to set. Samuel stood and turned to face the forest. He stepped in while clutching his sword and followed the setting sun. For hours he walked and glanced up. Peering through the tree tops to catch small glimpses of the sun.

The sun soon fully set and Samuel found himself in darkness. The sounds of the forest surrounded him; as well as sounds that could only be made by creatures not of this earth. Samuel kneeled down and took a piece of flint and steel from a small pouch on his belt. Setting a piece of char cloth on a small bundle of sticks Samuel struck a spark and made a small fire. It gave light to a small area around him. Just enough to give him warning if any creature came too near. Samuel sat for as long as possible next to the fire; staying on guard with his sword already unsheathed. But the heaviness of his eyes took him and he fell asleep. SNAP! A crack of lightning woke Samuel and a heavy rain fell upon him. He quickly stood as the wind howled sheathing his sword. "I need to find shelter." he thought. Samuel had to hold his arms up to shield himself from the wind and rain.

He walked almost blindly into the darkness of the forest. Then, without any warning, a large branch broke from a tree and fell on Samuel knocking him unconscious. As he laid in the mud, the faint sound of footsteps emerged through the pounding storm. A small man and woman stood before Samuel and lifted the branch from him. They grabbed him by his legs and dragged him away. After hours of unconsciousness, Samuel began to wake with the smell of stew filling his nose. Samuel opened his eyes to find himself in a small room with a round window next to the bed he lay in. He sat up with a groan as his head hurt from being struck. He reached for his head to find a cloth wrapped around it. As he looked, he found he was lying under blankets with only a tunic on. His boots, sword, shirt, and pants were gone. As he sat on the edge of the bed the door to the room opened and a small woman stepped through. "Ah you're awake." she said closing the door with her foot. She had a plate with a bowl of stew on it, steam rolling from the brim of the bowl. "How did I get here? Where are my belongings?" The women sat the bowl down on a night stand which sat next to the bed. "You were knocked out by a falling branch in last night's storm. Lucky for you my husband and I were coming back from our evening walk when we found you. We brought you here to rest. Your clothes were soaked with mud so I stripped you down and washed them. I'm sorry if the tunic is a bit small, but as you can see, we are dwarfs."

Samuels eyes widened as she said this. "Dwarfs? As in the creatures of old?" The woman laughed throwing her hands up in a jester.

"Creatures of old he says. Hahaha My boy we are very human, but you tall people think we are mythical in nature." Samuel sighed through his nose and apologized for what he had said.

"Eat your stew young man and we will talk more after." The woman stepped out of the room still smiling from Samuel's words. Samuel took the stew in hand and looked at it. It was a brownish stew with carrots, potatoes, and bits of meat. It smelled delicious Samuel thought, but he was still hesitant to try it. Though the woman told him she was human, Samuel had been raised to believe dwarfs hailed from the other realm. Still the hunger sat in his stomach like a rock and he took a spoonful of the stew. It was indeed just as delicious as it smelled. Soon Samuel found himself devouring the whole bowl.

Samuel stood after finishing the bowl and opened the door to the room. He found himself in a small cottage with a straw roof and large oak beams overhead. A hearth and fire sat opposite him with an iron pot hanging over it. The small woman was turning butter while sitting on a stool. She looked up at Samuel and smiled. "I see you liked the stew." she said standing up and taking the lid off the turn. Samuel thanked her for the stew and asked if he might have his things back. The woman said "yes" but to give her a moment to pour the fresh butter into a ceramic pot. Samuel offered to help her, although her and most things in the cottage were to her size, the turn was not. It was normal size and stood almost as tall as her. After putting the butter in the pot, the woman tied a piece of cloth over the opening and stood. "Now let's get you your clothes," she said wiping her hands off. "By the way young man, what is your name?" Samuel told her his name, and the woman responded with a smile, "That is a handsome name for a young man! My name is Magdalen; my husband is Allister. He was the one who helped me drag you here. He's outside pacing the yard. His mind is near gone due to his age, but I still love him and he keeps me company. Come! Your clothes are on the line drying."

Samuel and Magdalen stepped out of the small cottage. It sat in the middle of the forest with trees in all directions. Only where the cottage sat was there any clearing for light through the forest canopy.

Allister was standing. He was just as small as Magdalen with a long white beard that nearly touched the ground. Brown burlap clothes hung from his body. He was looking at a goose saying "Roll over doggie. Roll I say!" Samuel's face contorted to confusion and astonishment. He had heard of older people losing their mind but had never seen it. "I'm sorry for your husband Magdalen." Magdalen began to take Samuel's clothes from the line. "It's alright dear. I still love him and the man I married is still in there for now. He smiles at me from time to time the way he did on our wedding." Samuel nodded with a heavy heart. He looked back to Allister to see him trying to physically roll the goose. The goose honked and bit Allister on his big nose. Allister let out a yell and kicked the goose saying "You stupid dog!" The goose then opened its wings and started to chase Allister. "Run! The dog has gone rabid!" He said running for the cottage door.

Samuel held back a smile and swallowed it. Magdalen smiled and handed Samuel his clothes.

"You know, even though his mind is gone, he still brings a smile to my face."

Samuel looked at Magdalen with his eyebrows raised and a slight smile on his face. These people are not mythical. He thought. They are normal people living their lives and are happy.

"I hope one day society doesn't look on you as mythical." Magdalen smiled at Samuels remark.

"It doesn't bother us too much. We do well out here on our own; but I would like to be able to go to town and buy some things we can't make. Like new clothes or a new kettle for tea."

Samuel helped Magdalen take the rest of the laundry from the line and carry it into the cottage. After they were inside Samuel excused himself to the small room he was in before. He changed back into his clothes and put his sword on his belt. Samuel stepped back into the larger room while tucking his shirt into his trousers. Magdalen was sitting in a small chair knitting and Allister was also sitting in a chair and was tossing a ball of yarn between his hands. Samuel walked over to them and sat down on a stool. "So, tell us Samuel. Why are you all the way out here? Are you hunting?" Samuel cleared his throat.

"You could say that. My sister was taken by a troll during an attack a few days ago. She is the last bit of family I have left, and I must try to save her. I could never forgive myself if she is still alive and I didn't try. So, I'm on a quest to find her. I know trolls hide in the other realm because our sun is poison to them. Turns them to stone."

Magdalen stopped knitting and looked at Samuel. "You mean to go to Dreegahnna?" she said with an almost softness in her voice. Samuel looked with intent at Magdalen and said "What?" Magdalen looked at Samuel.

"The English call it a place of myth, The Irish call it Tír Na NÓg or Land of the Young; but it's true name is Dreegahnna and it is very real." Samuel listened with intent to Magdalen. "I know of it only through a trader that comes from there. Humans are not allowed there. Thankfully do to many associating us with them, Allister and I are able to trade with him when he comes. If you go there, time is different from here. A day there is a month here. That's how the fairy folk stay young to us."

"Samuel, your sister may still be alive, but it may prove impossible for you to get there. And even if you do, you may be torn apart by the fairy folk." Samuel looked to the ground and with a deep breath looked back to Magdalen.

"For family, I will gladly lay my life on the line." Magdalen sighed and sat down her knitting. She stood and went to a small box next to the hearth. She opened it and took a small ring from it. Turning to Samuel she held the ring up and spoke.

"A trader gave me this a while back. It can make the wearer look like the fairy folk, but you must never stand in front of a mirror. It can fool the eyes but not the reflection of one's self. If anyone sees your reflection they will know." Samuel stood and took the ring from Magdalen. He examined it as a child examines a toy. "Now there are a few things you should know before setting off. There are different types of fairy folk. Fairies look like people, but with a young glow about their skin and pointed ears. Many people think pixies are fairies but they're not. Pixies are small as an apple with wings and pointy ears. Leprechauns are the same height as us. I think that's why many people think dwarfs are mythical. But they also have pointy ears and are great shoe makers. However, they love to play tricks on folk. If you keep your eye on them, they can't disappear and will bargain so they could leave."

Magdalen continued "Selkies are human on land and sea lions in water. As long as they have their coat, they can shape shift, but take their coat and they are human. There are many more creatures, but I'm not too sure of them. You'll have to find out more on your journey. The last fairies you need to know is that of the fairies of death. The Banshee and the Dullahan. The Banshee will be near a body of water, like a stream, washing the clothes of the person about to die. Do not approach them or it will be your clothes she washes next. The Dullahan is the worst of the two though. A headless rider on a black horse or carriage. They carry their head as they ride. No gate nor door stays locked for them. If they see you one of two things will happen. You will either be struck blind or they will throw a bucket of blood on you. That blood marks you for death and they will speak your name. They can only speak once per ride. The name they speak is that of the person whom is to die."

Samuel swallowed as a chill went down his spine. His journey seemed more and more tiresome the farther he went. But his resolve was sound and his heart was true. He must do this to save Emily. Samuel looked back to Magdalen.

"How far am I from the gate?"

Magdalen took Samuels hands and said "Not but a couple hours walk from here. A large rock on a small glen is where you need to go. Before you enter, put the ring on; protect yourself Samuel."

Magdalen walked with Samuel to the door and stepped out. As they stood in front of the cottage, Samuel thanked her for her help and kindness and promised to return the favor someday. Magdalen hugged him and pointed behind him. "That is the way you need to go; good luck to you." Samuel hugged her again and was off. His goal was close at hand as he walked. A triumphant first step on his quest now filled him with pride. As he walked, the sounds of the forest filled the air. Birds chirped and the wind gently swayed the tree tops. The sky was clear with not a cloud in sight. But as Samuel walked, a sound started to emerge from ahead.

It sounded like metal clanging on metal. Was a blacksmith nearby, he thought? But as Samuel soon reached a small clearing, he saw that it was five men fighting someone with swords. A girl! Samuel grabbed the hilt of his sword and started towards the group. As he drew near, he saw it. Pointed ears. The girl had pointed ears; She was a fairy. Samuel stopped for a moment and thought. He might need to gain her trust if he is to travel to this Dreegahnna place. He took the ring from his pocket and slipped it on. Immediately his ears pointed and his skin became younger looking. Samuel was amazed at this, but he had no time to stand and revel in it. He had to help this girl. Samuel unsheathed his sword and pushed one of the men aside. He jumped to the girl's side with sword drawn and intent on his face. "Well!" said one of the men. "Looks like the little fairy girl has a fairy boyfriend. Boy, we were just after your girl. She would fetch a pretty price on market as a slave, But the two of you we could make a fortune. Not often someone comes across your kind."

Samuel responded "If you highwaymen truly think you can fight us, then have at thee!" The highwaymen laughed. The man who spoke before then said

"Alright. I suppose it's okay if we cut an arm off of you and take you." At that moment a rock flew at the man's face striking him on the forehead. The girl looked at them and spoke

"Enough of your talk. Men always gloat while fighting." With that, she lunged at one of the highwaymen striking his sword. As she swung her blade into his, she kicked the man in the stomach knocking him off his feet.

Samuel then went for the other men. His shorter sword made it easier to get in close to the men, as they had larger swords that gave them distance but not closer proximity. Samuel struck his sword to one of the men, but another man grabbed him from behind locking his arms. Samuel kicked as the man he was fighting now struck him in the face. Samuel reared his head back into the nose of the man who was holding him. The man let go as blood flew from his face. Samuel ducked another punch from the highway man and cut him across his back. The girl was fighting two other men as well. She threw dirt in one man's face and swept his legs from under him. She then stood fast and turned her blade to the other man. He struck high and the girl raised her sword to block it. But as she did, the man took one hand from his sword and threw a punch at her. She ducked by dropping to the ground, the punch missing her face by a hair. She then took the heel of her boot and kicked the man between his legs. The man dropped his sword and screamed.

Samuel was now fighting the man whom the girl hit with the rock. The large mark on his head from the rock bled. "Boy!" He shouted as their swords met. "I think I'm going to kill you and cut that little bitch's hands off. She can just be some meat for someone." Samuel threw a punch at the man's stomach, but the man absorbed it and kicked Samuel's legs, dropping him to the ground. Samuel swung his sword as he fell, hitting the man in his leg nearly taking it off. The man fell to the ground with a grunt. Samuel stood and put his sword to the man's neck.

"Tell your men to stand down!" The man looked at Samuel while holding his leg, blood pouring from the gash. "Lads!" The three remaining highwaymen stopped and looked. The girl breathing heavy as her sword was drawn to one of the men.

"These shits aren't worth our time. Someone help me up and grab Georgie's sword and coin purse." Samuel stepped back as one of the men picked up the wounded leader. The man whom the girl kicked between the legs held himself and grabbed their fallen comrade's gear. As the highwaymen limped away the leader turned his head and shouted,

"I never forget someone who's fouled me! I will find you again one day and have me revenge!" The girl then shouted back "Then bring men who can fight and not children!" Samuel sheathed his sword and looked to the girl. "Are you alright?" the girl sheathed her sword and brushed herself off.

"I'm fine. I've come here for years and never ran into humans. But I guess the stories are true about them. They are horrid creatures." Samuel gulped at her words. He knew he must stay in disguise. "I'm Samuel by the way." He extended his hand as he spoke.

But before the girl could answer a bright light came from a large rock behind them. Men in what looked like ancient Roman armor poured from the light. A man carrying a helmet under his arm stepped out from behind the soldiers.

"Your Majesty," the man said while snapping to attention and bowing his head.

"You had all of us worried. Your father is tearing the kingdom apart looking for you, yet here you are in the human realm." the man paused and looked down at the dead highwayman. "And fighting humans no less. Splendid. Your father will have my head for this."

The girl rolled her eyes a bit and said "Well maybe I like to come here and relax, and not be watched as if I am a fragile doll."

The man scoffed "Still, you should always be under guard. As our princess, you are next in line for the throne and if anything happens to you our world will be lost." The man stopped and looked at Samuel. "And who are you? Why are you with the princess?" before Samuel could speak the girl spoke for him.

"He said his name is Samuel. He helped me fight off some highwaymen but a few moments ago." The man pursed his lips and looked at the dead body.

"I see. Did you realize you had saved Princess Talia Dreegahnna?" Samuel was taken back by this revelation and replied "No. No I hadn't." *The princess?* Samuel thought. He had only helped because it was the right thing to do and that she might show him the way. Never had it crossed his mind that he was helping royalty.

"I'm not surprised..." said the man in armor. "The princess hardly attends royal events or public appearances. Many commoners have seen the king but not his heir." The girl brushed dirt from her hair and responded to the man in armor.

"Perhaps it is that I like my privacy away from the center stage. To not be doted over all the time."

"Your Majesty. When I was made Captain of the Royal Guard. My first duty was to protect, train, and see that you are ready for your future duties as queen." Samuel stood listening to the two debate one another. Rather than a servant of the crown being told what to do. It was as if the roles were reversed. Or at the very least as family speaking to family. Talia looked to Samuel.

"You'll have to excuse my protector Captain Rollins. He has been this way for years. Ever since my father told him to watch me every moment of my life." Captain Rollins huffed at the statement and then let out a sigh.

"Your Majesty. Ever since the war and the loss of your brother...." Talia looked at the captain with a glare which made him stop mid-sentence. "I'm sorry your Majesty. I overstepped." Captain Rollins then looked to the ground and cleared his throat. "We must be off. We are expected at the palace." Talia looked back to Samuel and said that if there was a way to thank him to name it. Samuel paused and said yes. He told her of his sister being taken by a troll, but he didn't say that she or himself were human. The fear of them either refusing help or killing him was present. As it was apparent humans were not well received.

Captain Rollins had a look of confusion come over his face. "A troll you say. The trolls have been exiled to the Black Mountains of the East. They are forbidden to come west anywhere near Dreegahnna. Tell me Samuel. How is it that your sister was taken by one? How did it get past the walls and army?" Samuel didn't know how to answer the question. To his knowledge, all mythical creatures just came from the same place. It never fully occurred to him that there were boarders and walls. Talia then spoke up

"This man has given me no reason not to trust him Captain. He did after all help me. If he says a troll took his sister, then I believe him." Talia looked back at Samuel. "Come with us to the palace. My father may be able to help. He loves all his citizens and hears them when they are in need."

Captain Rollins tried to object but Talia had none of it. She ordered one of the soldiers to open the portal so that they may return home. The soldier snapped to attention and said "Yes your Majesty." The soldier then turned to the large rock and drew the symbol of a Celtic knot. He then chanted in a language that Samuel didn't quite recognize. The ground shook and a light as bright as the sun appeared on the rock.

The soldiers walked into the portal. Talia took a step into the portal as well and motioned for Samuel to follow. Samuel was hesitant; he did not know what to expect on the other side of the light. However, he knew that if he was to save Emily he would need to go with Talia and the guards. Samuel stepped into the portal and Captain Rollins followed behind. Samuel found himself in a tunnel of light and color. The spectrum of lights twirled around him in all directions. It was beautiful in every aspect of the word. Soon Samuel found himself tumbling onto a grass flat land. Samuel stood to his knees and threw up. Talia looked at Samuel and smiled

"I see you don't use the portal that often. Many who do get sick the first few times they pass through. Well Samuel..." Samuel looked up and Talia continued "Welcome to Dreegahnna." A vast land of green and forest stretched before them. A large lake sat at the base of the hillside on which they were. Large snowcapped mountains sat in the distance and the Sun was cresting behind them. It was the most beautiful land that Samuel had ever seen in his life. It was here that Samuels adventure truly began, and here that his destiny would shape history.

CHAPTER TWO

Samuel was lost in the beauty of the land before him. Talia stretched her body by raising her hands above her head and arching her back. The soldiers were running into a column formation of two side by side. Captain Rollins was the last out of the portal. He, just like Samuel, almost vomited. Holding it back, he clutched his fist to his mouth and swallowed. With a clearing of his throat, he looked to Talia and Samuel. "Your Majesty. We brought a carriage for you."

The carriage sat on a small dirt road behind the soldiers. It was a wooden carriage painted in white with purple and gold trimming. At the front were horses, yet something seemed off about them. Samuel wasn't quite sure what but he knew something was different.

"Ah yes..." said Talia with a sarcastic tone. "The very tacky one. The one that announces to the land I have more wealth than them." Captain Rollins looked back to the carriage and then back to Talia. A look of astonishment on his face.

"Tacky? Your Majesty this is the second carriage the carpenters have built for you. They even included the colors you requested."

Talia let out a huff "I know. I just.... I don't like that some of our people are suffering on the fringes of the kingdom and we in the center of it have more wealth then needed."

Captain Rollins walked over to Talia and placed his hand on her shoulder "You have a good heart Princess Talia and you will be a great Queen one day. We have been sending as much relief as possible to the people on the out skirts, but we can only do so much." Talia grabbed Captain Rollins hand and took it from her shoulder gently.

"I know Captain. Tell the carpenters I will not require another carriage. This one will suit me fine." Talia replied with a heaviness in her words.

Talia then walked to the carriage with an almost sad look upon her. Samuel looked at Captain Rollins as he stood looking at Talia as a concerned parent would.

"She loves her people." Samuel said to Captain Rollins with a somberness in his voice.

"Yes, she does indeed." Captain Rollins put his helmet on his head and told Samuel to come along. Captain Rollins mounted a horse that was waiting for him. A large steed who was steady and strong from years of service.

"Samuel" Talia spoke from the carriage. "I would like to speak to you. Would you sit with me as we journey?" Samuel looked at Talia with surprise.

"Your princess has asked you to do something." Captain Rollins said with a command in his voice. Samuel swallowed and responded with "Yes, Your Majesty."

Samuel climbed in the lavish carriage. Its interior was a padded light purple wall and a dark blue bench on both sides. A small red curtain with bradded gold trim hung from the windows. "I have to say this is very lavish." Samuel said as he sat down on the bench opposite Talia.

Talia sat looking out the window to her right. Her arm perched on its ledge and her hand on her chin. As soon as Samuel sat fully down a whistle came from the coach driver and the wagon began to move. Talia still sat unmoved; her eyes seemed distant and focused as one would when thinking deeply. "Your Majesty?" Samuel said with a concern in his voice. Talia looked at Samuel with a slight turn of her head.

"I love this land. I love the people and the creatures that inhabit it. Since the war our family has done well, but many still suffer. I feel horrible when I walk into the towns on the furthest edge of the kingdom. I see people begging for food or coin. Children cradled in their parent's arms as the bite of winter touches their souls. As you said while climbing in to my custom-built carriage. It is Lavish" Talia said with a disappointment on her face. "I truly am disgusted that I live this way." Samuel sat listening to Talia with concern. Here before him was someone who truly cared for their fellow beings. Samuel started to speak with a softness in his voice.

"I can't say that I do relate to your plight your Majesty. I have only ever known hard labor. The thought that if I do not grow enough food for my sister and I then we may starve. That I must add new straw to the roof of our home before the next rain or winter. In those moments my thoughts are not on the strife of others but of my own." Talia slightly smiled and looked to the floor.

"I know that many are envies of my family for our life. It seems that we have an overabundance of food, coin, and protection from danger. It's not something that I really wanted in my life. But many people when they meet my father or I they grow happy. For many elders tell us that my grandmother saved them all from a fate worse than death. From slavery, true hunger, torture, and the lords of old. And that the last war was the finale end to the old ways of the land. That the trolls are no longer lords or that the goblins no longer take children to mine them new homes. That the dark magic that covered half the land has now gone. And the elders smile and sing our praise."

"They put us on a pedestal for what my grandmother, father, and brother had done." Samuel not sure of what to say or do in this moment leaned forward and placed his hand on Talia's hand and she looked up at Samuel with surprise.

"I think that if one cares as much as you do. Then they truly will be a great leader. For not many can say they feel the pain of their people and mean it." Talia smiled as a tear fell from her face. She took her hand from Samuel and wiped her eyes.

"I'm sorry to bother you with any of this. I normally don't speak to the people, so I'm not too sure what is fully appropriate to speak of." Samuel smiled and told her that she is welcome to speak to him at any time. Samuel then sat back on the bench and realized that he may have overstepped. Considering he is a normal person and Talia a royal.

"Forgive me if I overstepped in anyway your Majesty." Talia stopped Samuel and told him that it was okay. She loved that he showed kindness in listening to her and giving advice. Samuel then asked with a clearing of his throat.

"May I ask a question your Majesty?" Talia asked of what. "Why were you in the human realm?" Talia let out a small huff from her nose. "

I sometimes go to the human realm to be alone and think. I usually stay within the forests there. The clearing is a well-known spot in the human realm by the fairy folk. It's an ancestral place where the original fairy folk left the cruel world of man for the safe haven of here. Just as I was sitting there enjoying the quiet those humans attacked me. They must have thought I could grant them wishes or worse they would have used me as a plaything. Thankfully you were there to help." Samuel let out a slight chuckle

"By the way it looked. You could have fought them all on your own." Talia smiled

"Years of learning how to fight from my brother and Captain Rollins are the reason for that. They are some of the best swordsmen in the kingdom. Or rather...." Talia paused and a sad look came over her. Samuel then remembered that Captain Rollins had said Talia's brother had passed. Samuel thought quickly and changed the subject so as not to upset her further.

"I seem to recall that you and the captain have more of a family relationship rather than a princess and servant." Talia shook her head and snaped from her deep thoughts.

"Yes, I know it seems odd. You see Captain Rollins is... was a good friend of my brother. My brother joined the army against my mother's wishes. Of course, when father "the king" said yes. Mother had no more say on the subject. He and Captain Rollins trained with the Legions. Then the war broke out. Captain Rollins was with my brother when he died."

Samuel still wanting to learn more of this land listened with diligence. "What was the cause of the war?" Samuel asked to gather more information. Talia huffed and smirked

"I thought everyone knew the reason for the war. Well, when my grandmother Arina Dreegahnna liberated the land from the trolls. She was made queen of the liberated land and the trolls as well as goblins and dark magic users fled to the other side of the Black Mountains. They built arms and trained with what gold they took with them, and used slaves to fill the ranks of their armies. If a slave refused to fight, they or their family were butchered for the next meal. My father had been on the throne for only five years and my brother had just been made a Colonel. The trolls attacked and burned many villages on the rim of the kingdom. The wall wasn't even a thought then so there was no protection."

"My brothers Legion pushed too far too fast. The rest of the army could not keep up and they were surrounded. They fought to hold a small village in a wooded area. The town burned around them as a dark magic mage appeared. Captain Rollins and my brother fought hard. But dark magic is too powerful and Captain Rollins was badly injured. My brother charged and killed the mage only to be struck down by a goblin from behind. Captain Rollins swore that day he would protect our family and never let that happen again. I was very young when this happened. Old enough to remember the pain but not old enough to fight." Samuel bit his lip as he listened. This world of myth is to plagued by different ideology and beliefs. They to suffer from the follies of these creations.

"I'm sorry." Samuel said with empathy. "I'm sure your brother would be proud of the woman you have become." Talia thanked Samuel. A gesture of kindness that Talia had heard many a time before, yet this time it felt more sincere.

"I'm not sure if it is because you to are suffering the loss of a sibling or that you were willing to sit and listen to me blabber. But thank you Samuel." Talia then turned back to the window and began to think when a thought came to her. "Tell me" She said looking back to Samuel. "What were you doing in the mortal realm?" Samuel choked for a moment. He had hoped that this question would not be brought up again as it was with Captain Rollins.

"I... I was visiting a few friends." Talia looked at Samuel with confusion on her brow.

"Friends? In the human realm?"

Samuel thought quickly as Talia said this. "Yes. Friends. I know two dwarfs whom live not far from the clearing. They saved me after I was knocked unconcise by a falling branch during a storm. They gave me shelter and treated my wounds." Talia responded with a hum.

"You know the humans think dwarfs are one of us. That they are magical or have hidden gold like Leprechauns. Some fairy folk think this as well, but they are human. Just misunderstood. Mankind is foolish and think some of their own kind lesser just because of how they look. I pity and despise them for this." Samuel upon hearing this felt compelled to ask

"Why do you hate humans?" Talia raised her brow and took a deep breath.

"I don't fully hate them. Granted I do have a distain and as stated I do despise them, But I also pity them. There was a time when we lived with them. They respected us and we respected them. But they soon forgot about us. They started to destroy our lands and would try to capture us. It was nine generations ago when our ancestors had to flee to this realm. Some fairy folk still travel to the human realm, but it is very rare and yet they still have not changed as you saw. They still try to capture or destroy us."

Samuel then asked why she pitied them. That she didn't fully elaborate on that point. Talia leaned back into the bench and said she pitied them because they were lost. They used to live and let live but started to find ways to hate. Weather it was over how different someone looked or how much wealth they had. Talia looked at Samuel with a mixture of sadness and seriousness. "They forgot how to love. That is why I pity them." Samuel sat back and thought. What Talia had just said was true. He thought back to when the Romans left and how many tribes in his land fought to be in charge. How people were sold as slaves based on wealth or skin color.

"I think man may have taken notes from the Trolls." he said with a deep exhale. Talia huffed and said that wasn't possible, for man was doing these things before the trolls ever took power. The carriage soon started to slow and the coachman shouted

"Open the gate for her Majesty Princess Talia Dreegahnna!" Talia rolled her eyes and told Samuel they must have reached the city gates.

Samuel let out a slight laugh. "You really don't like being the princess, do you?" Talia rolled her eyes again and shook her head at the statement.

"It's not that I hate it." she said folding her arms "As I said everyone puts my family on a pedestal for what my family did and I don't like that. I have not done anything personally to help. I just send money and food to the poor and displaced. But nothing on the level my grandmother, father, brother, or even Captain Rollins have done." Samuel then replied with something that struck Talia in her heart.

"That is just as good as what they did. For it shows you truly care."

21

CHAPTER THREE

The sound of the carriage wheels clicked upon the cobblestone streets of the city. The sounds of people going about their day surrounded the carriage. Samuel looked out the window and was astonished by all that he saw. Creatures of all shapes and sizes walked the streets and shops. Many appeared to be fairies or fae folk, but included were leprechauns, pixies, and some strange animal/human hybrids. Samuel was amazed by the sight of all these different creatures. "Is this your first time visiting the capital city?" Talia asked.

"What?" Samuel replied as his mind was focused on the creatures and not the question.

"I could tell by the expression on your face that you have never seen these many beings in one place before." Talia continued, "I will admit it sometimes overwhelms me."

Samuel responded with a hesitation, "Yes... I've been to smaller towns, but never a large city such as this before."

Talia smiled and with a slight laugh told Samuel that the walls can be quite overwhelming at first. The carriage stopped again and the coachman shouted the same phrase as he did before. "Open the gate for her Majesty Princess Talia!" The carriage slowed to a stop and the door opened. A line of soldiers stood on both sides of the carriage door. They snapped to attention as Talia stepped out onto the cobblestone ground.

"This man is my guest and a guest of my father." Talia said to the soldiers. Samuel stepped out behind her and was taken aback by the castle that sat before him. It was a large limestone building with three large towers. A large center structure sat between the towers. The roof made of wooden shingles and arching windows with ornate metal work for support.

"Come. It is rude to keep his Majesty the King waiting." Captain Rollins said to Samuel with demand in his voice. As Samuel began to move, he glanced over to the horses on the carriage. Men were taking the reins from them when they suddenly transformed into people. Samuel looked with amazement at this.

The looming shadow of the castle stood before Samuel as he followed Talia and Captain Rollins. Two soldiers stood before a pair of large, wood and iron doors. As Talia and Captain Rollins approached, the two soldiers snapped to attention and opened the doors. The interior was almost as grand as the exterior. The floor was granite with pillars to match. The trim on the edge of the ceiling had an ornate design of flowers, twigs, and birds. Samuel stopped for a moment to take in the sight. It was the most lavish construction outside of a church that he had ever seen. To his left was a line of large arching windows, which over looked a large garden within the walls of the castle. The garden had a few trees and many types of colorful flowers. Stones laid in the ground making a pathway through it. To his right was a large wall with grandiose paintings of nature, and a few doors leading to rooms. Samuel proceeded through the hallway. His attention turned from the impressive architecture to the people moving within the castle walls. Servants were busy going to and from many rooms.

Some with brooms and feather dusters in hand, others with nothing at all. It certainly would take many people to keep this place clean and functioning, Samuel thought to himself. The hallway turned into a small staircase. Only raising slightly to a plateau with another staircase on each side. There before him sat another hallway that led toa set of large gilded doors. As the group approached the doors, two servants dressed in fine attire opened them revealing a grand room made of fine granite. Granite floors and pillars with slight marble texture and a deep blue rug with gold trim sat in the middle. Large arching windows allowing sunlight to beam in sat on both sides of the room. A small platform at the far opposite end of the room from the doors. Two grand thrones made of ornately carved red oak and fine fabric sat on the platform. A soldier stood every five feet at the position of attention leading to the platform. A spear grasped in their right hand and a shield in the left. Sitting on the thrones was a man in his sixties and a woman in her fifties. They both wore gold crowns akin to large rings and fine clothes made of satin. The man stood from the throne and crossed his arms.

"Talia, I swear you shall be the death of me. You were gone for near a week and your mother and I have been searching the whole of the kingdom for you." Samuel thought that it was different how this man was speaking to her. He was a king yet he spoke to her as a daughter and not with the grandeur that many royal families speak in his land.

"Father I was visiting the villages. Trying to help the people whom need it." Talia started to explain.

Before she could finish, Captain Rollins cut her off "We found her in the human realm your Majesty." Talia looked back at the captain as one would a younger sibling telling on the older.

"Father I..." she began to explain but was once again cut off.

"Talia, you know how dangerous the humans are. They are a filthy race that seek only for their selves. What if they had taken you? They may have made you a slave or worse." Captain Rollins interjected at that moment in the kings chastising.

"Your Majesty some bandits did try to take her. When we arrived, she had fought them off with the help of this young man here." Samuel's eyes widened and he stepped forward and bowed to the king. The king looked over Samuel.

"You saved my daughter and for that I am thankful, but tell me why were you in the human realm? It is forbidden to cross."

Samuel stood and thought quickly "I was trading with some dwarfs whom I'm friends with. They saved my life once and I bring them food from our land." The king glared at Samuel.

"Saved your life? That..." But this time the king was cut off by the queen.

"Young man. What is your name?" The king looked back to the queen with curiosity. The queen's eyes looked to the king and she said with a sly smile "Alaois you're so quick to condemn when a rule is broken.

He saved our daughter from human bandits. I think we can excuse him for visiting friends."

The king huffed and shook his head. He then turned back to Samuel "Well my boy. My wife and your queen has asked you a question." Samuel cleared his throat and told them his name. The queen smiled "That is a lovely name. Thank you for coming to my daughter's aid. As a mother I can never repay my debt, but as queen I can repay you with material goods. How can my husband and I do this?"

Samuel took a deep breath as his nerves were high. He was about to ask a favor of complete strangers whom hold great power.

"Your Majesty, I saved your daughter for it was the right thing to do. But I feel that it was fortune that I am now here. I was trading with my friends the dwarfs for a journey. My sister has been taken by a troll from the Black Mountains. I need your help to save her."

The great hall went silent. Many of the soldiers standing guard looked at one another with concern and confusion. The king looked intensely at Samuel.

"A troll took your sister?" the king said with a sternness in his voice "Your positive it was a troll?" Samuel responded with a yes. The king looked back to the queen with his mouth agape. "The treaty has been broken." The king said to the queen with a fear in his voice. The queen grasped a small locket around her neck and spoke

"We mustn't go to war Alaois. I will not put more mothers through the pain of losing their children." The king looked at Captain Rollins "Captain. How did they get passed the mountain pass gates and army?" Captain Rollins snapped to attention.

"Your Majesty I have had no reports of the gates being attacked. I was even there just a few days ago inspecting it when I received word to look for the princess. And to my knowledge there is no portal to the human realm in the mountains. So, they could not have come through the portal we returned through." The king then replied to the captain

"A tunnel then? Or has one of our men betrayed us?" Captain Rollins had the look of a child being scolded by his parents. Samuel's heart was racing as he heard the king speak with a sternly to the captain. The king turned to the queen and leaned in; bracing himself on the arms of her throne. He grabbed her head with one hand and put his forehead to hers. "I promise you there will be no war while I am king." he said with a firmness in his voice. The queen had tears in her eyes and she gripped the locket harder.

"I do not wish for Talia to be put at risk as her brother Tomlin was. His hair is all I have left in this small locket. Do not allow me to have only the hair of my daughter Alaois." The queen said holding back from crying completely.

The king then stood and turned back to the group.

"We will not go to war, but we will go to the mountains. Captain gather the Royal Guard I want the best men we have to come with us. A small platoon of sixty men. We will avoid war if we can. You Samuel, I will help you find your sister. If she truly was taken by a troll then she may be a slave. We will have to go to the slave markets in the town of Vera." Captain Rollins then spoke

"Your Majesty. Vera is on the other side of the Black Mountains on the Eastern coast. Even with the Royal Guard it is far too risky for you to come."

The king held up his hand and Captain Rollins stopped speaking. The king then said that he must come to ensure that no one will attack them and he can speak to the Lords of the realm peacefully on this matter. Captain Rollins bowed his head and said "Yes your Majesty." The king paced for a moment and said that they will need to prepare for the journey and that they will leave in the morning.

"Samuel you will come with us. If we find your sister there you may help point her out." The king looked at the small rusty sword on Samuel's side. "And you'll have a better sword then that." The king sat with a thump in his throne and placed his head in his hand. "The treaty stopped the war. We gave them our obsidian mines and part of our iron mines when they got the Black Mountains. We allowed them to keep the few loyal slaves they had just so they would never cross the mountains again."

"I did not want to let slavery remain in Dreegahnna, but the war and discontent would have continued if I had not. And we were running low on man power and food to sustain the war." The queen then spoke.

"A war cannot happen again Samuel. I hope that this is a misunderstanding and your sister has not been taken. I invite you to stay here for the night. I know the pain of lose and I wish for you to rest as I am sure you have had a weary heart and mind." Samuel paused and said that he could not accept such a generous offer since they are going to help him. The queen insisted though as it would be her way of thanking him for saving Talia as for helping him that was the thanks of the king. Samuel bowed with a thank you to the queen. The king looked up from his hand at Talia.

"As for you young lady. Though I know you are a capable fighter you are to stay here and are confined to the palace." Talia looked at the king with shock. "This is your punishment for leaving the realm." Talia objected to her father's punishment. The king held up his hand as his did with the captain and stated that he could have forgiven her traveling the country, but to leave the realm with no guard and come close to being taken. She can think over what she has done. The king called for his servants to enter the throne room. The doors opened to the great hall and a man and two women in fine attire walked in. They bowed before the king and queen. "This young man is going to be staying tonight. See that he is given a bath and a fresh set of clothing. As for my daughter take her to her room and lock the door until morning. Captain I want a guard at her door to ensure she stays there. Captain Rollins bowed and the group left the great hall. The male servant stopped by a set of stairs and held his hand to them.

"This way sir. We have a bath being drawn for you in your room." Samuel looked up the stairs. A large stair case that led high up into one of the towers. Samuel began the climb and took notice of the ornate designs carved into the banister. Stain glass windows looked over the courtyard of the castle. Paintings of people and great battles sat between them. Samuel thought of how grand this place was, but remembered on what Talia had said earlier.

There were people suffering in the kingdom and they live in luxury all for what her family has done. Samuel came from a family of farmers and was content with his life. Granted it was hard but they did not suffer. As far as he could tell the founder of this land Queen Arina did a great deal. Then Samuel saw a painting. A woman clad in armor atop a horse leading a charging army into a great battle against fowl beasts such as trolls, goblins, and sorcerers. This was Arina Dreegahnna at the moment she became legend. She looked almost like Talia but with a more broadness to her. Behind her was a man of thin build running with no armor and only a spear as his weapon. A woman with rags for clothing was flying slightly off the ground. Her hand and arm out stretched towards the enemy. The army that followed her was of farmers and people wielding clubs. It was not a proper army by any means yet with her leading them; They built a new land were Samuel now stood. "This way sir." the servant said jarring Samuel from his transfixed gaze.

Samuel took a final glance at the painting and proceeded up the stairs. The stairs soon gave way to a floor and Samuel found himself in a hallway. The servant opened a door to a room on his right and motioned for Samuel to enter. Tt was large with a small fireplace to the left side. A window and balcony sat opposite the room door with a bed adjacent to the right. A large copper bath tub sat in the middle of the room in front of the fireplace. Steam rising from the water and the faint smell of lavender wafted filled the air. The servant walked past Samuel to a wardrobe that was next to the bed. He opened the wooden doors and began sifting through several clothes. After a few moments the servant turned to Samuel and held up white shirt and brown trousers. "Here you are sir. I shall take your current attire and see that they are washed and sewn." The servant then looked at Samuel's boots. "I shall also see to your boots sir."

Samuel was not used to this kind of treatment. It was a treatment of nobility and he a farmer. "Please sir. If you would disrobe, I have many other tasks I must finish." Samuel snapped in surprise and looked to the servant for a moment. He then stripped his clothes from his body and handed them to the servant. The servant took Samuel's clothes and boots and left the room in a slight hurry. Samuel stood there for a moment to make sure the door was closed. He then turned his gaze back to the copper tub in the middle of the room.

Samuel thought back to how his bath at home was a wooden tub held together by iron bands; and how he and his sister would use the same tube to wash their clothes. Yet this fine tub before him was clearly meant for body washing and nothing more. Samuel sat down in the tub and the smell of the lavender forced itself into his nose. The water was a comfortable warm and not too hot. It brought a calmness to him and his tension began to ease. Though his mind was still on his sister Emily.

"She asked me to come with her. The field would have been fine for a few hours had I went with her." he thought to himself. The light of the fire place then caught the ring on Samuel's finger. *"The ring, of course."* It was because of the ring Samuel was able to come this far in his journey. *"I will need to find a way to thank Magdalen for this gift when I...."* Samuel's thought stopped.

He remembered what Magdalen had told him. Time worked differently in Dreegahnna; a day here was a month in the human realm. Samuel looked out the window at the setting sun. "I guess that's a month then." he thought. He then turned back to the ring and studied it. Nothing appeared to be out of the ordinary on the surface. Perhaps there was something on the inside. He took the rig from his finger with a tug. As the ring came off his finger his ears returned to normal and the youthful look he had left. His skin then became rougher and less smooth and the faint glow of magic left him. He was now back to his normal mortal self. Samuel took the ring and held it up to his face. There on the inside of the ring was a Celtic knot. Samuel remembered seeing the soldier draw this symbol when they entered the portal to Dreegahnna. What was it about this symbol that was so magical? How could this symbol have such power? CLICK! Samuel's eyes shot upward to the balcony window.

The windows opened and Talia stepped through into the room. Talia closed the windows and turned.

Her and Samuel locked eyes. A silence fell between the two as they stared at one another.

"Samuel.... You're...." Talia was cut off by Samuel saying he could explain.

Talia then pulled a dagger from her waist and pointed it towards Samuel. "Explain yourself! What is this witchcraft?!" Talia ordered. Samuel swallowed as he stared at the blade focused on him. He had seen and fought with Talia earlier. He knew that she was a great fighter and easily had the advantage.

"Well?!" Talia shouted. Samuel took a breath and began

"I am indeed human, but mean no harm. Please allow me to dress and we can talk this out peacefully." A tense moment sat between the two. Talia lowered her blade and spoke

"Only because you helped me earlier will I hear you out." Talia stepped back as Samuel stood up from the tub. Samuel covered himself with his hands. Talia looked to the fire and said "Please just dress yourself quickly." her face red with blush. Samuel stepped out of the tub and dashed to the bed where the new clothing was laying. He threw his trousers and shirt on quickly.

"There. All covered. I do apologize again." he said throwing his hands on his hips. Talia looked at Samuel, the dagger still clutched in her hand.

"Now explain to me. Why a human was using magic to hide. Were you trying to come here and gather slaves or treasure? Is the whole story of your sister a lie?" Samuel then cut Talia off with a firm "No" Samuel sighed and explained himself. He told her of how he was indeed looking for his sister and how he was given the ring by Magdalen. How he happened upon Talia in her moment of need and wanted to help her, but was afraid that she may only think him one of the highwaymen rather than an ally. As Samuel explained Talia slowly lowered her dagger more and more. Samuel soon finished hist story and sat down on the bed behind him. Talia looked at Samuel with anger and sympathy. Her mind was clearly puzzled by all that she had just heard. "But why did you help me? You had no reason to help." she said crossing her arms and leaning against the wall. Samuel huffed

"As I said. It was the right thing to do. I had no ulterior motive." Talia looked to the ground with her mind deep in thought.

"But humans are evil. They all only seek self-gain." Talia said under her breath. She looked at Samuel and demanded to see the ring. Samuel stood and held the ring out to her. Talia looked at the ring then at Samuel. With speed only matched by lightning Talia took the ring from Samuel's hand. She began to look at the ring and studied it hard. "I've never seen this work before. How did this make its way to the human realm?" she said while looking the ring over. Talia then turned with a swift motion back to Samuel, pointing the dagger at him again.

"I swear if you are planning any harm to my people or family, I will end your life." Samuel held up his hands and swore that he meant no harm.

"Princess if you do not trust me why is it that you felt compelled to tell me of your strife back in the carriage?" Talia lunged and pressed the blade to Samuel's throat, gritting her teeth. Talia and Samuel locked eyes for what seemed an eternity. It was in that moment of tension a knock came at the chamber door. The two looked at the door.

"Please I beg you. Do not reveal me to your father. I must save my sister Emily but cannot do that if I am sent back to the human realm or killed." Samuel said with fear in his voice. Another knock came at the door followed by a voice.

"Young man this is King Alaois. I wonder if I may have a word with you?" Talia's eyes widened

"It's my father." She paused briefly. "Fine. Take your ring and put it on, but this is not the last we will speak." Talia shoved the ring into Samuel's hand and raced to the window. Samuel put the ring back on hurriedly. At that moment the door opened and the king stepped in. Talia jumped from the balcony and hung from the railing.

"My boy I want to speak to you briefly." Samuel stood and bowed as the king as he walked into the room. King Alaois told Samuel that he need not bow every time he sees him.

"Yes, your Majesty." Said Samuel with a nervousness in his voice. King Alaois did not miss his nervous demeaner though. "I wanted to know more about how your sister was taken." The king said as he held his hands behind his back and walked around the room; observing all that he saw. Samuel took a deep breath.

"I sent her to market to sell some of our firewood and bring back bread. I was busy clearing our fields of stone so the harvest would do better and didn't go with her."

King Alaois paced the room "I see. And when she didn't return you went to look for her, yet found that a troll took her?" Samuel responded with a yes and that is what he was told by other people.

Samuel was doing his best to not trip over his words and remember all that he said earlier as well as not let the king know Talia was on the other side of the balcony rail. His fear was if he told the king, she was there she would tell him he was human.

"Samuel I still do not understand how a troll got passed my army or the walls. There is one road into the Black Mountains and it sits in a small pass. I would very much like to know these things and also know how you're positive it was a troll." Samuel re-explained himself to the king and stated he didn't know how the troll entered the land. King

Alaois walked over to Samuel and got very close to his person. "Look me in the eyes." said the king with a firm tone. Samuel looked into the king's eyes and short staring contest happened between them.

"Heavens. I see you are telling the truth but are hiding something else." King Alaois turned away from Samuel and walked towards the balcony; opening the windows and stepping onto the balcony. "Samuel, would you join me out here for a moment?" Samuel nodded at the king's request and stepped out onto the balcony. "I pray that your sister is not in the Black Mountains. The last war was bloody and took my son. The troll, goblin, and dark mage lords agreed to peace if we gave them an iron rich mountain and all of our obsidian, as well as the port town of Vera. They also demanded to keep slaves whom were brainwashed into being loyal to them. The very thing my mother escaped before forming this kingdom. I agreed on the condition that they cannot have anyone from this side of the mountains." Samuel looked at the king with unease.

"I made that deal to save the masses from more loss. Sometimes the few must suffer. It is a regret I will live with for the rest of my days." The king leaned on the balcony rail and sighed. "I worry that if the treaty has been broken, then I may see the downfall of this land or worse my only remaining child taken from me. That's why I forbid her from coming with us. If the trolls saw a chance to end my bloodline, they know very little would stand against them in retaking this land. No one would rally the people." Samuel leaned on the rail and could see Talia's shoulder.

"I think someone would rally people to fight. Your mother as well as yourself have shown people what it is to be free. And that anyone can rise if pushed enough. That idea is now inside of them and they will fight to preserve it." King Alaois stood and smiled at Samuel's words.

"My boy you may be right." King Alaois turned back to the window and started to walk back into the chamber. "Oh, and Samuel. Tell my daughter that if she is not in her room when I make it there, I will personally see she is locked in her room for a year." Samuel's eyes widened at the king's words. Samuel turned to the balcony rail and leaned over as King Alaois walked out of the room. Talia started to climb up and told Samuel to move. She stood on the top of the railing and jumped to another window pulling herself up into the window. Samuel watched in amazement of Talia's agility. Talia then leaned out the window and looked at Samuel.

"I will not tell my father since you did not of me. But I have many questions and that if you bring harm to us in any way, I will kill you." Samuel looked at Talia and took in her threat.

Samuel turned to the chamber and walked back in. The king was now gone and the room was empty. Samuel looked at the bed and sat down on it. He thought reflectively on today. Though these people were royalty they acted more of a family. Samuel thought of how his mother had died giving birth to Emily and how for years as children he resented her for it. It was only when their father fell ill that he started to understand the value of family. How he has tried for years to make amend to her. Samuel leaned over and placed his face in his hands. He lifted his head slightly so that his eyes peeked out of his fingers. "I swear if it cost me my life, I will save you Emily." Samuel laid back onto the bed. It was much softer than his straw bed back home. He stared at the light of the fire dancing across the ceiling. Its shadows making shapes of all sizes. Soon though Samuel's eyes grew heavy. Sleep was now upon him as he laid and his mind went blank.

CHAPTER FOUR

Thump! Thump! Thump! Samuel opened his eyes. The morning light filled the room with a slight haze. Thump! Thump! Thump! Samuel sat up and looked at the chamber door. "Yes?" he said wiping the sleep from his eyes. The door opened and a female servant walked in.

"Sir his Majesty King Alaois Dreegahnna requests your presence post haste outside. If you would follow me sir." Samuel stood and thanked the servant.

Samuel then stopped her from leaving with a gesture.

"Miss, I hope this isn't to forward. Why do you and many others serve the royal family." The servant bit her bottom lip and closed the chamber door.

"Sir, it is not forward at all. Many people have asked me that same question before. Some of us work for the Dreegahnna bloodline out of gratitude for all that they have done. Others work out of necessity to provide for their families." Samuel then asked why she worked for them. The servant girl smiled at the question. "I work for them because the king saved my family during the war. He and his men rode into our town as it was being sieged. Our house was set on fire and I and my mother and father were trapped. The king and his men rushed into our home and dragged us out. Right as they pulled us out a small group of goblins and slave soldiers attacked them. The king fought like a hundred men and held them off. The entire time he cried "Save the people!" I cannot forget that." Samuel took in this story with admiration of the bravery.

The servant girl then curtsied and left the chamber. Samuel took a step and felt the cold floor beneath his feet.

"My boots. That's right the man last night took them to be cleaned." Right as Samuel said this the chamber door opened once again. A small man near only three feet in height walked in.

"Ah glad I caught ya." he said taking a sack from his back. "I've been working all night on these poor things. You've gotten yur use from them. But I was able to make them look new." The man opened the sack and pulled out Samuel's boots. They were a clean shining black leather. Samuel looked at them and paused.

"Those are not my boots." The small man laughed

"Ah but they are. Many of us Leprechauns take pride in or shoe making. I replaced your soles and tacked a new heal on. They should last ya a few more years if ya keep them." The leprechaun handed the boots to Samuel. Samuel was amazed at the transformation his boots had went through. They no longer looked as worn and ragged as before. "Well, boy I must be off. I'm glad ya like the work I've done." Samuel thanked the leprechaun and bowed his head. As the leprechaun started to leave, he paused. "I almost forgot. The servants found this gold coin in the pocket of yur pants. They asked me to return it to ya." The leprechaun turned and flicked the coin to Samuel. Samuel caught it in his hand and remembered what the bartender had said to him. To keep this coin on him at all times. "Oh, and lad." Samuel looked up at the leprechaun "I won't ask how ya got it. But don't let people know ya have a human realm coin. The servants didn't realize it but I did. There are people who would kill a man just for having something from the human realm."

Samuel's heart seemed to skip as the leprechaun told him this. "Take care boy." With that the leprechaun left the room. Samuel thought of what was just said to him. "There are people who would wish to harm or kill me just for having a coin? But why? It's just a harmless coin." Samuel gripped the coin in his hand and felt his determination build. He was given this coin for a reason and if it helps him save his only remaining family then so be it. Samuel tucked the coin into his boots and put them on. He made his way down the winding stairs that he had climbed the night before. The sunlight poured in through the windows that lined the stairs. There was not a spot of darkness anywhere. Samuel hurriedly walked down the stairs. Captain Rollins stood at the bottom of the stairs.

"Ah. I was just about to come and see if you were awakened by the servants. His Majesty is waiting on us outside with the horses. Here, I had a sword taken from the armory for you." Captain Rollins held up a small sword with a polished brass hilt. Its sheath was a polished steel; giving a mirror like shine.

"Thank you, Sir." Samuel said as he strapped the blade to his waist.

"Samuel I still have questions about your trip into the human realm. Granted you may have been there visiting some dwarfs as you said, but I didn't become Captain of his Majesties Guard by trusting the word of everyone."

Samuel paused at Captain Rollins statement. Then with a quick thought he responded "I have nothing to hide. I mean no harm to anyone and my only intent is to save Emily from the troll who took her." Captain Rollins glared at Samuel.

"Then I suppose we shall have to learn to trust you through your actions. Come, we are keeping the mission and his Majesty." Captain Rollins turned and began to walk down the corridor. Samuel thought of how Captain Rollins did not trust him. Maybe he is right not to. After all Samuel was lying about who he really is.

Samuel followed Captain Rollins to the courtyard that they had arrived in the day before. There in the courtyard was a platoon of sixty men on horseback. They wore chain mail armor and steel helmets. A shield sat on their backs and a short sword hung from their waists. As Samuel and Captain Rollins stepped out everyone snapped to attention. It was then the King Alaois stepped into the courtyard. The men on horseback drew their swords and held them in front of their faces. The horses then did something Samuel had never seen before. They stepped a leg forward and bowed to the king as he walked past. "Your Majesty" Captain Rollins said bowing his head. Samuel snapped back to the king and bowed as well. "I have assembled sixty of our best Royal Guards. As well as sixty Pooka Dragoon. If we should encounter any problems, they will transform and fight next to us. Granted they would be naked, but they all have a blade strapped to their stomachs and skill to use them.

That makes one hundred and twenty men able to fight." As Captain Rollins explained this to the king Samuel studied the word Pooka.

He felt he had heard that word before. Yes of course he has. A Pooka was a creature half human and half beast. The most common legend being of them as horses. Samuel remembered stories he would hear from the older town's folk as a child. King Alaois studied the men then addressed them.

"We are going into the Black Mountains on a diplomatic mission as well as a possible rescue. This man here is named Samuel. He saved my daughter from bandits and I am granting this mission as a thank you. He claims his sister has been taken by the Troll aristocracy. If true we will need to save her and leave there as quickly as possible. Samuel, please tell us what your sisters name is and what she looks like." Samuel walked in front of the soldiers.

"Thank you all for helping me do this. My sister's name is Emily. She is five and a half feet tall with brown hair." It was then Samuel realized. Emily was still human and these men would be trying to find a fairy girl. Samuel knew that he must find her first before these men do. If what the leprechaun told him was true. Emily may be killed by these men just for being human. "She...

She is light in complexion. Thank you again." King Alaois looked at Samuel.

"It is okay my boy. Not everyone is meant to speak to a large group, but every detail you gave us will help." King Alaois held up his hand and gestured to a stable boy to bring his horse. "Samuel, I want you to ride next to me in column. Captain you will ride at front and guide us to the boarder." Captain Rollins looked to Samuel and told him that he must keep watch over the king and guard him with his life. King Alaois laughed and said it maybe he saves Samuel as years of fighting had made him a skilled blade. The king then looked to the men and ordered them into a column of four. With a mighty shout of acknowledgement to their king. The men hurried into a column of four men side by side and fifteen deep. Samuel stood in amazement at the professionalism of these men. King Alaois took note of Samuel's face "I see you admire the swiftness of my men. The Royal Guard are some of the most well-trained men we have. In total only one-thousand of them are in the Royal Army, and the

Army is eight-hundred thousand strong." Samuel then turned to King Alaois with curiosity.

"Your Majesty, why is it your other guards wear armor of steel and these men wear armor of mail?" Captain Rollins then asked the king if he may explain. King Alaois told Captain Rollins by all means as he climbed upon his horse. Captain Rollins nodded to the king and turned back to Samuel.

"We have the Royal Guard wear chainmail armor because it allows for better maneuverability in battle. These men train every day they are on post with wood swords and real shields. They fight with their fists while in armor to practice if they lose their sword in battle. I along with veterans of the war devised this training method so as to prepare them for future war. All their training is based on the experiences I and many others had during the war." Samuel was impressed with the captains reasoning behind the soldiers intense training. Though he has never served he did understand the need for a well-trained army.

"Gentlemen" the king said with a thunder in his voice. "Please mount your horses and let us be off. The day is short and the ride is long." Samuel and Captain Rollins acknowledged the king and took to the horses that were waiting for them. Samuel had little experience riding a horse and it took a moment for him to take to the mount. Captain Rollins watched Samuel struggle to his horse.

"I thought as much." he said to Samuel "You've little experience on horseback. To go forward give a gentle kick with the heel of your feet. To go right pull the reigns to the right same for the left. To stop pull back both sides slowly." Samuel studied the reins as Captain Rollins explained. Samuel thanked the captain for his advice. "Just please don't fall from your horse. I do not wish to carry your broken body back here." Captain Rollins then rode his horse to the front of the column. Samuel rode his horse next to the king whom was already in the center of the column. Once Samuel was in place Captain Rollins shouted to the guards in the gate house of the castle. The men shouted back in acknowledgement and both ran to a large wheel that had a crank on it. They turned the wheel allowing it to make a clicking sound. The large iron gate on the castle walls lifted upward and two large wooden doors opened outward.

Once the gates were opened King Alaois shouted "Guards of the Royal Army! Proceed!" The column then started moving forward. Samuel gave a gentle kick with his feet and the horse let out a small whinny and jerked forward. King Alaois laughed at the sight. "My boy it will take some time for you to become better at riding." As the column rode through the gate Samuel was finally able to see the full scope of the city that sat outside the castle. The buildings were well kept and the streets were clean and full of people. As the column rode down the main street a crowd of people began to gather.

They cheered as the king and his men rode by. It was then the column came to the city sqaure and a large fountain sat in the center with a twelve-foot statue of Arina Dreegahnna. In her left hand she held chains with a collar and in her right was a sword. At her feet sat a plaque which read "She freed herself from the chains of slavery and liberated us all by giving us a home." The surrounding builds were all shops of different trade. A baker, a butcher, an apothecary, a book store, and many more. Samuel turned to King Alaois and asked

"Your majesty. What was Queen Dreegahnna like?" King Alaois smiled at the statement.

"She was much like how Talia is now. She had a determination about her. A fire in her soul that no one could smother. I take heart in that Talia is like her but at the same time my mother had something Talia does not." Samuel asked as to what that was. "My mother knew how to be patient. I was born after the War of Liberation. My father was taken by an assassin when I was a babe. My mother still found time to raise me during the building of the kingdom." Samuel then asked what the first years of the kingdom were like. "It was troublesome. Though we were free the Troll Aristocracy, the Goblin Regents, and the Dark Mages sought to end us. Attacks on cities and towns were common. It was then decided by my mother to erect walls around the major cities and towns and they would be protected by veterans of the war. She then declared that all homes will grow their food in small gardens behind them. All meat will be provided by the hunters for one gold coin a pound." Samuel stated that it must have been difficult the first few years. King Alaois nodded and said it was indeed but they had help from the few good mages in the kingdom. Samuel then remembered the floating woman in the painting of the battle.

"I saw a woman in a painting on the stairs leading to the room you allotted me last night. Was that one of the good mages?" King Alaois then got a serious look on his face.

"She was my mother's best friend and helped found the kingdom. Her name was Áine. She was one of two of the most powerful mages in the world. She lost someone important to her and though she was warned by Grand Mage Mcclaney. She tried to bring him back from the dead."

Samuel was shocked at the statement. Was it possible for that to happen? If so, why had they not tried to bring back Talia's brother? "Your majesty, how did she do that?" King Alaois paused briefly

"She tried to use dark magic. I was fifteen winters when she tried. The north tower of the castle exploded after a green light had been coming from it. Her body was never found. It is assumed that she was destroyed by it. After that my mother banned dark magic in the kingdom and restricted light magic. She said it was too dangerous to use." Samuel then asked if the magic had worked. King Alaois huffed at the question. "If it, had I saw no proof. You know Samuel, everyone is born with darkness in their hearts. Some embrace it, some suppress it, and others stay unaware of it all together. Dark magic feeds on the darkness in one's heart. The darkness in her heart at that time was the unbearable loss of a loved one. Her one and only child."

Samuel listened to the king's story with intent as they rode to the outer city gates. "The few mages whom used dark magic in the kingdom fled to the Black Mountains and the lands beyond. The troll's offered them protection from my mother and her forces." Samuel still trying to find out as much as he could about Dreegahnna had questions abound. His natural curiosity could not help but fill his head with them. But he knew prying to much may draw more attention than wanted to him. The column of men soon reached the outer city gates. The stone walls stood higher than the ones of the castle by at least a few feet. Captain Rollins shouted for the gates to open for the king and his men.

The large gates opened and the column moved through. As the men left the city walls behind them. They entered into a type of countryside with large fields and farms surrounding the area. Forests, hills, and mountains sat in all directions.

The road on which the column traveled had become a well-traveled dirt one. A large ditch sat on both sides of it to allow for rain water not to wash it away. The ditches had cuts in its sides to allow water to flow into the fileds and help water the crops.

"I may need to use your techniques of ditch digging to help the yield of my field back home." Said Samuel observing the fields. King Alaois let out a slight ha and spoke

"I was a bit curious as to your profession. A farmer is it then?" Samuel smiled at the statement and said that it is not an important job and that he only provides wheat for the neighboring town. King Alaois retorted at Samuel's words. "That is the most important job for any population. A people cannot survive without food. The hunters and butchers provide the meat, but the farmers provide the food for the animals as well as the people. Without people like you Samuel an echo system of a community or nation would suffer. Take pride in your work."

Samuel had never fully thought of his work that way. He had been doing his work simply to provide for he and Emily. But now that he had been given clarity about his work. He could take solace in the fact that he is necessary to the town. The column came to the edge of a large forest that sat a few miles from the farm lands surrounding the castle. Though the forest was dense beams of light found their way through the tree tops. Darkness seemed to not show at all in this forest. The dirt road laid before the column in a straight path. Captain Rollins shouted to the column

"Men be mindful of the forest. A wolf may lurk in the calm of the field." King Alaois shouted back to the captain

"I fear not the wolf captain, I fear only a man whom waits." Samuel was thrown by this statement. What did the king mean by it? Samuel asked the meaning of such a statement. King Alaois explained that it is an old military term. It is wise to fear the enemy before you or the one in hiding, but much

wiser to fear the one that does nothing and plans. As the group moved through the forest. Samuel took note of a few ruined structures that lined the sides of the road. Over grown with vine and weed and a tree or two bursting through them. Like pillars holding the roof of the forest. A peaceful calm seemed to radiate from them. Samuel took these ruins as the remains from the last war. As from what he could see the faint sight of scorch marks remained on some of the stone work. The group rode for hours in the forest and soon sun set was upon them. Just as it seemed the column would be sleeping in the forest for the night. They came out of the forest into a clearing. There in the clearing was a village. It was a quaint village of only a few dozen buildings and a few roads seemed to enter it from all sides.

The homes were a combination of wood, stone, and concrete. It was rustic and the appearance of small carvings on the buildings gave rise to questions in Samuel. The carvings were that of men with axes and saws. "Was this a village of carpenters or loggers?" Samuel thought. The column entered the village to find few people out as many were going home for the night. It was then that a town guard noticed the column and ran up to them. He had no armor but rather a tunic with an axe on it. A sword hung from his waist and a helmet with chin strap undone sat upon his head. The guard brushed himself off and he bowed to the king. King Alaois looked at the guard and asked "Is the lord of the town here or is he away?" The guard said that Lord Cillian was at his home in Charwood Hall in the center of the village. King Alaois asked that the guard go and make his presence known and that he requests an audience with him. The guard bowed ran away to the center of the village. Captain Rollins ordered twenty of the men to ride ahead to the home Lord Cillian and make sure it is secure. Twenty men broke from the column and followed behind the town guard.

As the column waited for confirmation of Lord Cillian expecting them. People began to take notice of the king and his men. Soon the few people that had not yet entered their homes for the evening came to great the royal entourage.

Many of the people bowed to the king and some of the children whom had come out to see the troops gazed and spoke in admiration of them and their armor. The soldiers smiled and one even took a child and placed them on his horse. The child smiled and began to pet the horse while giggling. Samuel knew of the admiration the king had from the people, but this was a new experience that he had not seen. A level of love and respect that few will ever know in life. It was at this moment that the town guard whom greeted the king and his men returned.

Out of breath he announced to King Alaois that Lord Cillian of Charwood will great him and his men at Charwood Hall. Captain Rollins looked at the heavily breathing guard and said that he should focus more on his fitness in his free time rather. "How is a town guard charged with the protection of the people to maintain order when he can barely run less than a mile?" He said with judgement. Captain Rollins then ordered the column to proceed. As the column moved through the winding streets people could be seen looking from the windows of their homes.

Some would open the windows and cheer as King Alaois rode by. Children would watch in admiration and cheer for not just the king but the soldiers as well. The column soon found itself in the center of town. A grand house sat to one side of the square. It was that of wood and stone with plasterer of white. Dark wooden shingles adorn its roof and arching windows filled with light looked at the square. The Royal Guards whom had rode ahead stood at attention outside of the house. As King Alaois and his men approached the front door of the house opened revealing a warm light from within. An older man near the same age as the king stepped out from the home.

"Your highness" he said with his arms wide and a bow "It has indeed been a long time since you have graced us with your presence. What took you so long?"

Samuel was taken back by the comment. Here was a man whom just gave a slight insult to King Alaois. "What will the king do?" He thought to himself. King Alaois smiled at the comment and replied

"Lord Cillian your smell has kept me away, but I had heard you had finally bathed."

The lord stood and began to laugh. King Alaois then stepped down from his horse and embraced the lord with a hardy hug. The two men laughed for a moment then King Alaois told the lord of why they are traveling through his town. Lord Cillian looked over to Samuel.

"My friend I am sorry for your loss. But I am sure his majesty will help you find her." Samuel thanked Lord Cillian for his kind words as his dismounted his horse. King Alaois asked if he and his men may rest for the night in Charwood as they had been ridding all day. Lord Cillian replied "Of course! Your majesty is always welcome in Charwood Hall. Your men may sleep in the guest quarters. Come in and let us feast for the evening." Captain Rollins ordered the Pooka Dragoons to change to their mortal forms and go wash before entering the lord's house. All sixty horses then changed into men. They were sweaty from a day of ridding and carrying the other soldiers on their backs. The Pooka dragoons then hurried into a large bath house that sat next door to Charwood Hall. Samuel watched still in amazement that there were beings whom could change form like this.

As King Alaois, Captain Rollins, Samuel, and Lord Cillian began to enter Charwood Hall a man on horseback came ridding hard into the town square. "Your Majesty!!" He shouted as he rode hard to them. Before his horse could fully stop, he leaped from its back and handed King Alaois a letter. He opened it and began to read. Captain Rollins asked the ridder why he was riding as hard as he did to catch them.

"TALIA!!!" shouted King Alaois to the group of solders whom were standing outside. "I know you're here young lady. Now step forth." The soldiers began to look at one another and all around in search of the princess. It was then that a soldier from the back of the group stepped forward. The soldier removed their helmet revealing shoulder length hair. It was Talia dressed as one of the Royal Guards. She approached her father the king slowly. As she did, she handed the helmet to Captain Rollins and spoke

"You may wish to train your men better. I was able to knock this one out and take his armor." Captain Rollins looked at the helmet and then at Talia in shock. King Alaois then began to chastise Talia as an angry parent would.

"I told you to stay back at the castle and yet you blatantly disregard my order." Talia then spoke against her father in response.

"Father I am not a child. How am I to rule one day if I do not come on missions of diplomacy with you?"

The king began to get angry but at that moment Lord Cillian interjected.

"If I may your majesty? Your daughter does indeed have a point." King Alaois looked at Lord Cillian with disbelief. "But your father is also right princess. He only ordered you to stay out of love. Please let us all come in out of the night air, rest, eat and discuss this calmly." King Alaois looked at Talia and replied

"Very well. Let us enter." The group entered the home with Lord Cillian at the front and King Alaois behind him. Servants thought fewer than at the royal castle stood and bowed as the king entered. The interior of the hall was made of craved wood. Animals of all kind stood in the carvings staring down at the group as they entered. A well-made red carpet lay under their feet. To the sides of the carpet were slivers of walnut flooring. A walkway hung to both sides above the group's heads. Room could be seen on the walk way. Large hand carved support beams hung far overhead. It was a home for someone with power but it wasn't as well made as the king's castle.

Samuel was still impressed by all that he was seeing. The homes and life styles has seen while being in Dreegahnna are far greater than the life he lived. The group then came to a grand hall made of stone with a large table still being set by servants. The table overlooked the hall from a small stone platform. A large stone fireplace sat to the right side of the hall and windows sat high above slightly obscured by wooden beams.

"Please if you will. The high table is now set for you and yours your highness. I shall see to it that a few more tables are set for your men."

Lord Cillian said with a smile. King Alaois stepped onto the stone platform and sat on a chair at the center of the table. Talia sat down to his left and Captain Rollins to his far right. Leaving a set open for Lord Cillian. Samuel began to sit at a smaller table on the dining hall floor with the Royal Guards. "Samuel" King Alaois said echoing the hall.

"As a guest of the king you may sit at the high table." Samuel stood and thanked King Alaois and approached the table. The only remaining seat at the table was to Talia's left. Samuel sat down with his heart beating near from his chest. He worried that Talia may at any moment expose Samuel as being human, but she did say that she would not. Samuel tried to calm himself by this fact but the unnerve remained. Talia looked from the corner of her eye at Samuel.

"I will speak to you later." she said with a whisper. Samuel looked at Talia and took in her statement. King Alaois then began to speak to Talia

"Talia, I told you stay home for your safety. If you die by my side your mother will be destroyed with grief." Talia looked at her father and said that she will not die. That she has spent years learning to fight and now must learn to conduct diplomacy. King Alaois sighed and placed his hand upon his forehead. Rubbing it as one would a headache. "My heavens, I will never be able to protect you with your zeal for life." Lord Cillian returned to the hall and stepped next to King Alaois.

"Your majesty and men of the Royal Guard. As my guests I offer you a feast." Lord Cillian than sat in his chair next to the king. A door on the far side of the dining hall opened and servants came out with trays of bread, cheese, and sliced meat.

Lord Cillian looked to King Alaois and apologized for not being better prepared for his company. Or he would have had a better selection of food. He also explained that a hog was being roasted as they spoke and it will be done within the hour. King Alaois thanked Lord Cillian for his generosity. The soldiers began to eat and servants came around with tankards of ale. A servant approached King Alaois with a bottle of wine and a silver chalice. Lord Cillian stood and took the bottle of wine and chalice.

"Your highness, allow me to pour your glass in friendship." King Alaois stood and took another chalice made of bronze in hand.

"And allow me to pour yours in fellowship." The two men took the bottle of wine and poured it into the chalices. They then locked arms and took a deep drink of the wine finishing within seconds. Samuel remarked to Talia

"I have never seen such a custom." Talia turned to Samuel and explained that Lord Cillian fought next to her father in the war. That they are brothers in arms and do this as a sign of respect for one another.

"Many men of the war have a certain way of greeting one another and wishing them well." Talia said as she slumped in her chair and crossed her arms.

King Alaois looked at Talia "Now to show appreciation for this feast. I would ask my daughter to sing a song for us." Talia's eyes widened at the statement. She turned her head to her father with a look of shock and surprise. "Talia please. We are guests here and I know Lord Cillian as well as myself would enjoy a song. You used to be such a wonderful song bird when you were younger." King Alaois lowered his voice to a whisper

"And you can accept this as your way of apologizing for disobeying my order." Lord Cillian replied with a hardy smile

"Splendid! Bring forth the minstrels to give the song a tune!"

Two men entered the hall one with a drum and the other with a flute. A soldier stood from the Royal Guards and said that he had on his person a small fiddle and another then stood and said he had a tambourine. King Alaois laughed and told the soldiers to join in with the minstrels. Talia huffed and stood, she looked to her father and asked what song he wished to hear. King Alaois scratched his beard and told Talia he wanted his favorite song of all to be sung. Talia sighed and looked to the minstrels. "Dulaman, please" Talia said as she stepped onto the hall floor. The minstrel with the drum then gave the beat. As the group began to play many of the soldiers whom were sitting began to chant with it. "Dulaman, Dulaman Gaelach. Dulaman, Dulaman Gaelach. Dulaman, Dulaman Gaelach." It was then that the minstrel with the flute began to play. Talia with her heart beating began to sing a song of beauty that Samuel had never heard. A song of another language foreign to his ears. Samuel began to tap his foot to the song. Many of the soldiers slightly drunk from the ale started to dance with one another and a few of the servants. Lord Cillian bowed and held out his hand to a servant girl whom was standing close to him. She smiled and curtsied to the lord taking his hand. The words of Talia's song then filled the hall. "*A 'níon mhín ó, sin anall na fir shúirí. A mháithairin mhín ó, cuir na roithléan go dtí mé. Dúlamán na binne buí, dúlamán Gaelach. Dúlamán na farraige, be'fhearr a bhí in Éirinn.*"

Samuel had never heard this song before, but he could tell it was one of joy. King Alaois clapped his hands and tapped his foot. But he himself was over taken by the music and began to dance in the style of river step. Many of the servants whom had been serving food and ale joined in as well and Charwood Hall was alive with life and joy. Talia's distain for singing began to melt away as she saw the joy that had come over the hall. The song continued to flow from her as joy soon began to fill her. "*Tá ceann buí óir are an dúlamán gaelach. Tá dhá chluais mhaol are an dúlamán maorach. Bróga breaca dubha are an dúlamán gaelach. Tá bearéad agus triús are an dúlamán maorach. Góide a thug na tíre thú? arsa an dúlamán gaelach Ag súirí le do níon, arsa an dúlamán maorach.*

Rachaimid chun Niúir leis an dúlamán gaelach." It no longer felt as a punishment but rather a pleasure. She herself began to sway to the music and a smile soon formed on her face. Talia turned and looked back at Samuel whom was now standing and clapping his hands.

Their eyes met and the world seemed to fall away. Though Talia knew that Samuel was human. She in that moment was only taken by the joy that her song was bringing. Samuel stepped down from the high table and made his way to Talia. Samuel then held out his hand and asked "Dance with me?" Talia whom was still singing thought upon the question. "*Ceannóimid bróga daora are an dúlamán maorach. Ó chuir mé scéala chuici, go gceannóinn cíor dí 'Sé'n scéal a chuir sí chugam, go raibh a ceann cíortha.*" With a slight hesitation she took Samuel's hand. The two began to spin and dance franticly as many others in the hall were. Samuel and Talia began to smile wider at one another. Talia's suspicion began to give way and Samuel's fear of being exposed began to fade as well. "*Cha bhfaigheann tú mo 'níon, arsa an dúlamán gaelach Bheul, fuadóidh mé liom í, arsa an dúlamán maorach. Dúlamán na binne buí, dúlamán Gaelach. Dúlamán na binne buí, dúlamán Gaelach.*" In that moment they were not skeptical of one another but rather happy to be living in that moment. Talia took Samuel by the wrists and spun him in a large circle and let go. Samuel fell back onto a bench at one of the tables. He looked up at Talia who smiled with a slight laugh. She then jumped from the floor to a table top behind her and with a grand finish the minstrels and Talia concluded the song. "*Dúlamán na farraige, be'fhearr a bhí, be'fhearr a bhí. Dúlamán na binne buí, dúlamán Gaelach. Dúlamán na farraige, be'fhearr a bhí, be'fhearr a bhí Be'fhearr a bhí in Éirinn!!*"

Many people in the room though out of breath began to cheer and gave a standing ovation to the princess and minstrels. Kinga Alaois laughed and smiled applauding his daughter.

"My sweet daughter I see your voice has not faded. Bravo, bravo." King Alaois looked over to see Lord Cillian sitting down on a chair. Sweat pouring from his brow but a smile that shined brightly upon his face. King Alaois laughed. "I see though you are younger than I. You are the one whom is about to pass from exhaustion." Lord Cillian chuckled at the king's statement.

"Older and fitter you may be. But more well fed and out of shape am I." The two men laughed at each other. King Alaois then looked to the minstrels and asked that they play another song. The minstrels bowed and began to play a more slowed jig. A few of the soldiers tapped their feet but no one danced as they had just a moment ago. Servants whom had been dancing bowed and curtsied to their partners and went back to work. Talia stepped down from the table top and made her way back to her seat. Samuel, King Alaois and Lord Cillian followed suit. Lord Cillian took note that Captain Rollins had not joined in the fun.

"Tis the matter Captain?" Lord Cillian said while giving a slap on Captain Rollins back. "Unable to dance?"

Captain Rollins let out a ha and said that he has never been one for dancing. Lord Cillian laughed as he took his seat. "Then we must find you a woman whom can show you." As everyone took their seats the servants entered the hall with a large roasted hog on a palankeen. It was larger than any Samuel or for that matter anyone had seen. King Alaois looked at Lord Cillian with surprise and asked how his cooks prepared such a beast in only an hour. Lord Cillian laughed and took a drink of wine from his challis. "The right heat, the right seasons, and a bit of light magic. Our cook was once a light mage, but he said his true passion was cooking. I tasted his food two winters ago in the market and gave him a job on the spot." King Alaois motioned his head with an ah ha and looked back at the hog being brought before them. Samuel was in shock at the size of the beast. It was the size of a horse and near as fat as a wagon. Talia looked at Samuel and asked

"Have you no hogs as big as this on your farm?" Samuel replied with a no. That he and Emily only had a few chickens and raised wheat. A servant stepped before King Alaois and bowed. He then produced a knife and began to carve the hog.

A large slice was given to the king and Lord Cillian. Talia asked that a smaller slice be given to her. Samuel received a slice near as large as the kings and Captain Rollins asked for a slice of shoulder. Another servant then came with a pot full of potato stew and scooped a helping onto their plates. King Alaois then stood and held his challis up in a toasting manner.

"Men of the Royal Guard and Pooka Dragoon. I wish you to have this hog and fill your bellies with it." The soldiers cheered at the king's words. Talia began to cut her food when she took notice of a window next to the fire place. A small child was looking into the hall. The child was as thin as bone and covered in dirt. It was then the child took notice of Talia and ducked below the window. Talia motioned for one of the servants to come to her. The servant bowed to Talia as they approached. Talia leaned forward in her chair and told the servant.

"There is a child outside who looks hungry. Please take them some food and this." Talia produced a small leather purse full of coins from her pocket, handing it to the servant.

"You really are kind hearted you know?" said Samuel watching Talia. Talia slightly turned her head to Samuel and replied that she has a kind heart for her people, but still has little trust in humans.

Samuel looked at Talia with a look of disappointment. Taking a breath and a drink from his challis. "Then why did you accept my offer to dance but a few moments ago?" Talia leaned back in her chair

"Because I was caught in the moment of joy. I...." Talia paused momentarily thinking of her words. "I want to speak to you later when we are alone." Samuel looked at Talia with curiosity.

"Very well. Are you planning to end me?" he added taking another drink. Talia took a bite of her food and wiped her lip.

"I would have done so sooner if that was the case." Samuel smiled and nodded at Talia's words. Samuel looked over to the window to see the child that Talia had sent food to being greeted by the servant. A smile came over the child's face as a plate of food and the coin purse was handed to them. Samuel observed the act of charity in happiness and admiration.

Though Talia acted strong and brave she had a gentle soul beneath her skin. As the night went on and the guests of Charwood Hall filled their bellies. The once lively hall soon fell silent and many of the soldiers passed out where they had been sitting. Lord Cillian stood and looked to King Alaois

"My friends I feel as though I cannot eat anymore. We have feasted and drank our fill from my pantry. I bid you a goodnight and offer my finest rooms for you all." King Alaois stood and took Lord Cillian's wrist in brotherhood.

"We need not your finest but a bed that is soft and warm." Lord Cillian tiredly smiled at King Alaois.

"If you follow me your highness. I will show you the chamber close to mine. Servants, see that Princess Talia, Master Samuel, and Captain Rollins are given beds." Captain Rollins interjected that he was going to retire to the bath house next door before going to bed. He stood from his chair and bowed the king and lord. Then without another word he stepped down from the high table and walked out of the hall. Careful not to step on any of the soldiers whom were by this time snoring on the floor. King Alaois followed behind with Lord Cillian and a servant stepped before Talia and Samuel. The servant bowed and asked that the two follow him to their rooms. The pair followed the servant out of the hall and up a small set of carved wooden stairs. The railing of which was an ash branch with its bark removed. As the trio reached the top of the stairs a small walkway with rooms to the right lay before them. To the left was more ash branch railing and pilers of walnut. The servant stopped and held out his hand to one of the doors

"This room is your Master Samuel. Yours is next door your majesty." The servant bowed as he said this and then excused himself.

Talia and Samuel were now alone standing outside of Samuel's room. Talia opened the door to Samuel's room and told Samuel to enter. Samuel thought for a moment and did as he was asked. As soon as he was fully inside the room Talia stepped in behind him and slammed the door shut. She then slid an iron lock in place on the door and looked at Samuel.

"You and I have much to discuss. You told me why you are here and what your quest is. But I want to know things only you could answer."

Talia then grabbed Samuel's wrist and held his hand up

"My first question is how this ring found its way to the human realm." Talia threw Samuel's hand and released him. Samuel rubbed his wrist and looked at Talia.

"I told you Magdalen gave it to me to hide the fact I'm human. She said a trader gave her the ring a long time ago. Why are you concerned with it?" Talia glared at Samuel.

"That ring holds a magic that has been banned by my grandmother. It is dark in nature and only if someone looks closely can they see that. You humans are blind to magic and would not recognize light nor dark unless told."

Samuel looked at the ring on his finger. It seemed normal in all aspect to him. Samuel looked back to Talia "But if I were evil would you have not discovered me?"

Talia huffed "Evil can sometimes hide in plain sight. And humans though I pity them have only proven to me that they are as I have been told. One bad apple can spoil the bunch and all of you have been rotted." Samuel looked in slight disappointment at Talia.

"Not every human is evil. I'm sure it is like that here as well with your people." Talia replied to Samuel's statement.

"Maybe but I'm sure they are far and few in number." Talia paused for a moment and said that she wants Samuel to come with her to see someone. Samuel became confused and asked whom they were going to see and when. For they were setting off in the morning for the Black Mountains. "Master Senan is the most powerful light mage in Dreegahnna and he lives an hour ride from here. We will sneak out in a few moments and go to him." Samuel took in Talia's solution and agreed. He then crossed his arms and leaned on the wall behind him.

"Until then I am sure you have other questions your majesty." Talia immediately answered Samuel with a yes.

"How did a troll take your sister? My father was right in saying no portal exists in the Black Mountains. Also, for what reason would a troll leave our realm just to take a human?"

Samuel threw his hands slightly upward and said he did not know how nor why. Only that Emily was taken and many were killed in an attack on his village.

"Maybe your mage can tell us something when we see him." Talia paced and responded that maybe Senan could. After all he was the most powerful mage in Dreegahnna and knows all magic. Samuel then asked Talia if he may ask a question. Talia shook her head and flung her hand in a yes gesture as she paced the room.

"How do you know this Senan and if he finds out I am human will he not try to kill me?" Talia stopped and looked at Samuel.

"He is more likely to examine you rather then kill. He has always been fascinated by humans. For what reason I do not know. And I know him for he was the mage whom helped my grandmother found the kingdom." Samuel paused at the statement and asked, "I thought the mage Aine were the one whom helped your grandmother." Talia paused then replied.

"Yes. Senan trained Aine in light magic. She was the only person in the kingdom whom could rival him in power. But after she was killed Senan became the only powerful mage in Dreegahnna." Samuel then asked if he was that old how could he still be alive? Talia explained that a mage can trap part of their soul and strength in a crystal to extend their life.

She wasn't sure of the exact magic used, but that many mages use this method to extend their life. "It is as if their bodies slowly taken in the strength from their souls in the crystal to and extend their life." Samuel though confused at Talia's explanation responded with

"Ah. I see." Talia was quick to recognize Samuel's loss.

"Don't bother trying to understand. As I said magic is lost on humans." Samuel smiled and slightly laughed at Talia's words.

"You really do have little faith in us humans." Talia stopped pacing and gave Samuel a glare.

"How dare you. To stand here and insult me like this." Samuel just smiled at Talia's anger and replied

"If I have given insult then is it not fare? You have been slighting humanity the whole time I have known you."

SMACK!

Talia struck Samuel across his face. She then walked over to the door unlocked and opened it. In a harsh low tone, she told Samuel to meet her outside in five minutes. Talia then slammed the door as she exited the room. Samuel still smiling rubbed his cheek.

"If that was a slap, I would hate to have a punch." Samuel shook his head and walked over to the chamber window. He opened it to take in some air before he ventured out of town with Talia. Samuel leaned on the window ceil and looked up at the crescent moon. The sky was clear and many stars shined brightly with a purple like heugh dancing across the sky. Samuel was taken in by the comfort that it brought. He then turned his attention to the roof tops of the village. They were a mix of straw and wooden roofs. Samuel could see the edge of town where a timber mill sat on a small stream. A giant water wheel powering it's might blade. Not too far from the mill were large dirt mounds with smoke pouring from them. "Charcoal furnaces. So that is why this place bears the name Charwood." Samuel said as he looked out. Many of the homes in Charwood still had light coming from their windows. A calm seemed to emanate from the entire village.

Samuel then noticed movement below his window. He looked down to see the bath house from earlier. Captain Rollins was coming out of the bath house. A robe was all he wore and a servant followed behind him with his armor and sword. A soldier walked up to him and saluted by balling his fist and placing it over his heart. Captain Rollins then took a letter from his robe pocket and said something in a low voice to the soldier. Samuel observed in silence at the transaction. "What are you sending and to where?" Samuel muttered. The soldier saluted the captain again and walked away. Captain Rollins told the servant to follow him and the two entered Charwood Hall. Samuel was not sure of what he had just saw but felt a seance of unease. He stood and closed the window drawing the curtain.

Samuel thought that he should ask Talia when they ride together. Maybe she would have an answer about Captain Rollins. After all she had known him her whole life. Samuel walked over to the room door and opened it. He leaned his head out and made sure the way was clear. Samuel felt as a child sneaking up past bed time doing this, but he and Talia needed answers. Samuel slowly exited the room closing the door behind him. Samuel tip toed quickly down the stairs. When he reached the bottom, he heard laughter coming from his left down the corridor. Samuel looked to see a solider smiling and talking to one of the servant girls. She was laughing at his words and the two both had a tankard of ale in hand. Samuel took the opportunity while the two were laughing to make his way to the door. Samuel quietly opened the front door of Charwood Hall. Two soldiers stood guard by the door. One looked at Samuel and said asked what he is doing. Samuel thought quickly and said he was stepping out for some air. The soldier nodded and went back to being on guard. Samuel fully stepped out of the hall and onto the street.

The only life in the village seemed to be him and the soldiers. Samuel walked over to the stables which where adjacent to the hall. The stables were made of wood and stone with a straw roof. A lantern hung on a post in front of the stables and a small gate hung next to it. Samuel entered the stable to see many of the Pooka Dragoons sleeping on piles of hay.

Many of them now wearing clothing but all clenching the swords that Captain Rollins gave them. Samuel made sure to step quietly making his way to his horse. He came close to waking one of the dragoons but thankfully the dragoon rolled over and did not notice Samuel. Samuel slowly patted the nose of his horse and opened its stall door. It was one thing for Samuel to sneak in but now he must navigate his horse out of the stable. He very slowly leads the horse past all of the sleeping dragoons. The horse came close many times to waking the dragoons. It almost stepped on one of their hands even. But with patience Samuel managed to get the horse out of the stables. Now though Sameul faced a new problem. How was he to get his horse past the two soldiers standing guard in front of Charwood Hall. As Samuel looked around the very small corner of Charwood Hall he could see the soldiers standing guard. It was at that moment Talia jumped down from the roof of Charwood Hall on to the soldiers. She grabbed their heads and slammed them into the ground knocking them out in an instant.

Samuel became shocked at the sight for he was impressed and her agility once again. Talia stood and noticed Samuel spying on her.

"Come. My horse waits for me." She said turning away from Samuel. Samuel followed Talia to the other side of Charwood Hall. Her horse stood tied to a lantern post next to the bath house. Talia untied her horse and mounted it and spoke

"Come on. We don't have all night to waist. We will go quickly and quietly until we get out of the village."

Samuel nodded and mounted his horse. Talia and Samuel took their horses into a quick trot. Thankfully the dirt streets of Charwood were not stone. For instead of the clicking of hooves on stone only a small thump gave credence to the riders. As soon as the two exited the town Talia slowed her horse. She looked to Samuel and said that they should be far enough outside town to begin a full gallop to Senan's home. Samuel replied

"Lead the way your majesty. I will be close behind. I want answers too and maybe he can lend us a hand in finding Emily."

With a call and a snap of their heels Talia and Samuel darted into the night. The dirt road wound through the forest opposite where they had entered town earlier that day. A small stone bridge sat across a stream and gave way to a large meadow. The moon illuminated the whole meadow and glinted off of the water in the stream. Fireflies flashed their lights across the tops of flowers and trees. Even as the two rode a calm seemed to live across this land.

"There! Senan's house on top of the hill!"

Talia called out to Samuel whom was ridding behind her. Samuel looked to see a large two-story house stood saluted atop a nearby hillside. A small stone wall wrapped itself around the base of the hill with a winding road leading up to it. The house had a stone base with oak logs holding the corners. The roof was made of wooden shingles and the windows of a slightly bubbled glass. A large stone chimney stood high next to the house bellowing smoke from its peak. Talia and Sameul slowed their horses to a walk; the horses breathing hard from the ride. Talia and Samuel dismounted their horses and tied them to an iron loop hanging from the stone wall.

The two began walking up the hillside to the house when a voice came seemingly from the air.

"Princess Talia, my, my how you've grown." Samuel looked around to find the source of the voice but to no avail.

"Old man we need your help." Talia said with a joking manner.

"Oh, you have always been as brash as your grandmother was. And who is this at your side? He does not look like one of the Royal Guard nor a servant of the palace." Samuel still looking around for the source of the voice addressed Master Senan's question.

"My name is Samuel. Princess Talia and I have come seeking your help..." But before Samuel could finish Master Senan interjected.

"Young man I feel a dark magic coming from you. It is faint but there non the less. Speak of why you stand with the princess and choose your words carefully. I know when someone is lying to me."

Samuel swallowed at Master Senan's words and could not even mutter a single sound. Talia noticed Samuel's fear and spoke in his place.

"Master Senan, that is why he and I are here. We need your help."

A silence fell over the quaint hill; Talia and Samuel stood looking to the house with baited breath. The wooden door to Master Senan's house then opened and the warmth of its interior flowed over Talia and Samuel.

"Come in then and let me see that which troubles you."

Talia and Samuel entered the home and the door closed behind them. The interior of the house was massive. It seemed larger inside then outside did. A large stone fire pit sat in the center of the house. A wooden stair case sat to the right side of the room and gave way to a wooden platform that rounded the home. The center of the platform did not connect in the rooms center. Allowing Talia and Samuel to see the upstairs portion of the home. Shelves of books stood soundly on every wall. A chair covered in blankets sat next to another fire place to the right of the room.

A small iron pot hung over its embers from a bar built into its hearth. An arching window of stained glass sat opposite the door Talia and Samuel had entered. Allowing the light from the moon to gleam in the home. Samuel looked upward to find that a map of the star and their constellations hovered overhead. But this was not a map of paper nor paint. It was as if the night sky itself was inside the home.

"Master Senan? Where are you?" Talia asked looking around the home. Footsteps began to come from the platform above and a figure soon began to come down the stairs. An old man whom was bald on top of his head and had a long snow-white beard and mustache that stretched almost to the ground came walking down. He wore old worn brown leather shoes and a raged red tunic held in place by a rope around the waist. He was hunched in stature but if stood up would be a man of six foot. The old man paused and looked at Talia and Samuel.

"Princess I don't know why you are accompanied by one with dark magic, but if he has hurt you in any way."

Talia replied to Master Senan and said that it was not Samuel whom had the magic but the ring he carried. Master Senan fully came down from the stairs and shuffled over to Samuel. He looked at Samuel from top to bottom and walked all around. Samuel followed the old man with his head and had a puzzling look on his face. Master Senan then grabbed Samuel's hand and held it up to his face; looking intently at the ring.

Master Senan then pulled the ring from Samuel's finger turning Samuel back into his human form.

"I knew it." He said with excitement "I could tell you were human the closer I looked. No magic is a challenge for me, but tell me mortal why you have come to our land and how you procured this ring of darkness."

Samuel told Master Senan the story of Emily being taken and how he ventured forth to find her. It was when Samuel's story reached the names of Magdalen and Allister that Master Senan stopped him

"These dwarfs. Describe them to me."

He asked sitting down on his chair by the hearth. As Samuel began to describe Magdalen and Allister to Master Senan; the old man waved his hand and two comfortable chairs appeared behind Talia and Samuel.

Master Senan gestured for the two to sit down as Samuel continued. "I knew it." Master Senan said stroking his long white beard.

"Those two are of fae origin and come from this realm." Samuel was surprised by Master Senan's words and asked how that was possible. That they were both mortal in appearance. Master Senan nodded to Samuel's words and replied

"You see Magdalen and Allister are leprechauns and it was I that made them appear mortal." Talia looked to Master Senan confused and asked why he would do this. Master Senan waved his hand by the hearth and the flames grew in size. "Look into the fire and see what my memory holds." There in the flames Talia and Samuel could see figures take shape and voices soon began to flow from the images. A woman sat on a bed crying heavily. A rag held tight in hand and her hair a mess. Samuel leaned in and looked closer at the figure.

"I know her." Samuel said pointing to the figure. "That is the woman I saw floating in a painting in your castle princess." Master Senan nodded and said that the woman that they see in the flames was Lady Aine.

"My one and only pupal, and adopted daughter. Same as I adopted your grandmother princess."

Talia asked why she was crying and where she was. Master Senan let out a harsh sigh and said that Aine had just lost her child whom was not a year old.

"You see Aine fell in love with a soldier whom was killed in a raid on the newly made boarders of the kingdom. Before he died, he gave her a son whom was born with no problems. But sometimes we can be blind to problems; at only ten months the child died from a bad heart. This is Aine when she had just lost the poor dear."

It was then a knocking sound came from the flames. Aine raised her head and said for whoever it was to go away. A voice came from behind a door

"Lady Aine her majesty wishes to come see you in a moment." Samuel took note of the voice and said that it was the voice of Magdalen. Master Senan nodded and told Talia and Samuel to watch the flames. Aine wiped her eyes.

"Magdalen please tell the Arina I do not wish to see anyone right now." A small pause came between the two. Then Magdalen replied

"Lady Aine ya have not eaten in four days say for some water. Please eat something and as for her majesty she is coming up the stairs now." No sooner had Magdalen finished and a knock came at the door.

"Go away Arina! I just want to be left alone."

Aine shouted as she fell back onto the bed curling into a ball. A voice then came from the door

"Aine please; We are concerned for you. Master Senan is even here to see you."

Aine waved her hand and the room door opened. Queen Arina Dreegahnna stood in the doorway older than what she was in the painting Samuel had seen. Talia asked Master Senan how long after the kingdom was formed that this had happened. Master Senan said that it was twenty years after the rebellion had concluded. Samuel asked how Lady Aine was so young looking as compared to the queen. Master Senan smiled and spoke

"The same way I am sitting here now telling you this. Aine had put her soul into a crystal to extend her life. She wanted to be around for a long time for her son after her lover was killed." Samuel thought of Master Senan's words and then asked how old he was. Master Senan smiled and replied that he was old enough.

"Aine please." A voice said in the flames. Samuel turned back to the fire to see Queen Dreegahnna sitting down on the bed next to Aine.

"If I could turn back time and change things I would. But it has been four days and you have not eaten. We are all just concerned for you."

Aine continued to lay facing away from the queen. It was then Allister walked into the room. Not the disheveled man that Samuel knew, but a well-dressed and cleaned man. His ears were pointed and he wore a vest of green plaid pattern with three brass buttons. A pair of burgundy trousers and black shoes with a brass buckle on the top. Samuel upon seeing Allister muttered

"He looks much better here than when I met him."

Master Senan replied with an ah and said that this was before Allister lost his mind. It was then that Magdalen walked into the room behind Allister. She looked similar to how Samuel had known her only slightly younger and carrying a tray with bread, an apple, a cup of water, and some sliced meat. Master Senan then stepped into the room looking no different in age but his clothing was of better make then that he was sitting in. Master Senan the placed his thumbs in his trouser waist and spoke

"Aine my sweet child I have searched my books and found nothing. I wish I could offer my help for I hate to see you in such a pain." Aine turned to everyone standing in her room.

"You are all so kind, but please leave me."

Queen Dreegahnna perked her lips with a frown and patted Aine on her shoulder.

"Aine we are leaving the food and water for you. Please eat something and gain your strength."

Queen Dregahnna then stood and motioned with her hand for everyone to leave the room. As everyone did Allister looked at Aine whom was still lying on her side looking away from the room door. Allister let out a sigh and placed his thumbs in his vest arms. He walked around the bed to the front of Aine.

"Allister go away please."

Aine said with tears flowing down her cheeks. Her green eyes blood shot with heart break. Allister held back a frown and told Aine that he may know a way to help her. Aine wiped her eyes and said that there is no way to help. That she had traveled to the land of the Dullahan and asked them as well as the Banshee to give her child back.

"They all told me No. They said that once a life has left this world it can never return." Allister inhaled deeply and replied

"That's not entirely true Lady Aine. I know of a fellow whom I saw myself get stabbed through the heart. He was dead as stone and yet he walks now. If anyone knows the secret to coming back it is him."

Aine looked at Allister with confusion and asked how it was possible. Allister said that he wasn't sure but he did know where the man spent his leisure time. Aine sat up on the bed and asked Allister where this man was. Allister told Aine that the man could be found almost every night at a tavern outside the castle walls.

"He sits at a table by himself; You'll know him when you see him."

Allister then nodded and looking to the ground he walked out of the room. Aine sat thinking of how this could be possible and many other questions roared through her head. The flames then swirled and the image of Aine disappeared. Talia asked what was happening. Senan told her to be patient and that he was skipping ahead to when Aine met the man. Samuel then asked how Senan could know what happened when Aine met the man. Senan huffed and spoke

"I began to watch her after her child had passed. Grief can make someone do things they may normally never do. It was for her safety." Samuel sat up in his seat

"You spied on her?"

Senan nodded and said that he did it out of love and care for Aine. The flames then showed the image of Aine walking into a tavern. Many patrons paid no attention to her as she was wearing a cloak. Aine looked around the tavern which hung low with smoke from men's pipes and only the light of candles and a fireplace broke the haze. There sitting in a corner of the tavern was a man drinking a tankard of ale. He was slumped back in his chair against the wall of the tavern. His clothing was of darkened leather studded with silver embellishments.

Aine approached the man as he took another dink. He looked up at her; setting his ale on the table before him.

"Lady Aine" the man said in a rough graveled voice. "To what do I owe the honor of you coming to me?"

Aine paused and asked how the man knew who she was. The man laughed and said that a good mage can tell when another is near.

"And here I thought you were the best in the land only behind Master Senan."

Aine looked over the man and felt a strange presence emanating from him.

"You're a dark mage."

The man laughed at Aine's statement

"Oh yes I am and non-too pleased with how your little rebellion forced many of us to die or flee." Aine sat down on a chair opposite the man.

"Then why are you still here and not either of the former?" The man took a drink and cleared his throat with a grunt

"Cause I enjoy the ale here and I like to keep my enemies closer than my friends. So, will you answer my question now? Why are you here to see me? Do you wish to kill me or banish me?" Aine leered at the smugness of the dark mage and leaned in with her elbows on the table.

"I heard that you had cheated death." The man took a slow drink from his tankard and looked at Aine through the top of his brow.

"Aye, That I did. I heard of your child and give you sympathy only in that. I take it that is why you are here?" Aine looked at the tavern patrons and waved her hand. The room froze in time with her motion and a silence filled the room. The man looked around the room and took another drink. "Now that is a trick even, I don't know."

Aine looked back to the man and said that if he told her how to bring the dead back, she would teach him her spell. The dark mage laughed at Aine and finished his ale. He then stood and walked over to the bar grabbing a bottle from the shelf behind it.

"Even if I wanted to show you how I could not." he said pulling the cork from the bottle. Aine stood and looked at the dark mage

"And why is that? Do you hold a grudge against me for the war?" The man took a drink from the bottle and said that he did have some contempt for the war but that was not the reason why he could not show her.

Aine walked over to the dark mage and grabbed his wrist, stopping him from taking another drink.

"Then tell me who can?" The dark mage set the bottle down on the bar and looked over Aine from head to toe.

"I can tell you who can, but there is a price. Nothing is free in the world."

Aine took a bag of coins from her waist and slammed them down on the bar. The dark mage looked over the coins and said that would cover him telling her who to speak to but not the spell. Aine grew angry at the mage and demanded that he tell her. The mage took a drink from the bottle and told Aine that there is a spell to contact the one she needed to speak to. He then took a small scroll from his breast pocket and handed it to her. As Aine took the scroll in hand the dark mage held tight and spoke

"Once you do this, there is no going back."

Aine took the scroll from him harshly and turned away. As she started to walk out of the tavern; she waved her hand and time unfroze. The image again faded from the fire and a new one began to form.

"Why didn't you try to stop her?" Talia asked.

Master Senan said that he did try to stop her, but he was too late.

"She had barred the door leading to her tower and placed a spell upon it. Only her and Allister were in that tower when it exploded. Queen Dreegahnna and I tried to break the spell on the door so I don't know what happened up there.

Sadly, Allister was found on a nearby roof with his mind warped. Whatever they saw in that room was enough to destroy his mind."

Samuel then asked how his ring fit into all of this. Master Senan nodded and said that anything that was in that room became filled with darkness.

"I found the ring and noticed a spell on it that would allow one to appear human or if a human wore it, they would become fae. Magdalen wanted to take Allister to where they would be left at peace; away from the world of magic."

"She asked for me to make her and Allister appear human so they could be left alone. I used my magic to do so and though there was darkness in that ring it is not harmful in such a low state. I gave them the ring as remembrance of our land and if they ever wished to return to wear it and find me. But it seems she felt you needed it more."

Master Senan leaned forward in his chair and handed Samuel the ring.

"Young man you have come to a land wear your kind is not welcome. Though you said your sister was taken by a troll I dare say she me be dead and you have endangered yourself by coming."

Samuel put the ring back on and a listened to Master Senan's words. Samuel looked back to the old wizard and said that Emily was his last remaining family, and if his life is forfeit to find her then so be it. Master Senan stroked his beard and looked over to Talia and asked

"You say your father along with some men have agreed to help young Samuel?" Talia slumped back into her chair with her arms crossed.

"Yes, though I question his motives or if his sister even is real." Samuel looked at Talia with shock.

Master Senan sensed the tension and asked Talia why she was being so hostile to a person that she was helping. Talia became irritated

"He lied to me! I thought he was fae and here he is a human. Then he had the audacity to be smug in every conversation." Master Senan raised his brow and nodded

"Tell me princess. Has he not done anything to warrant your trust?"

Talia grew silent for a moment and said that he did save her from some humans who were trying to take her, and that he had shown compassion on many subjects they spoke of. Master Senan smiled.

"Then perhaps you are more taken in by preconceived notions simply because he is human. I was but a babe when the fae left the human world. My mother told me of how the humans would constantly try to take fae folk hostage for gold or magic. But she also said there were many who respected the fae. She even saw a family bow before her and others as they passed by. That whole notion of one bad apple spoils the bunch only applies to apples. There are many good humans as well as bad just as there are many fae whom are bad and good."

Talia calmed listening to Master Senan. She looked away from Samuel and Master Senan at the fireplace. Master Senan then turned to Samuel and said that he has been given a great privilege to be the first human in centuries to enter Dreegahnna and he should not be so smug. Samuel let out a soft sigh through his nose and turned to Talia

"I'm sorry. I do care for your people and their struggles, but I guess I was being rude to your hospitality." Talia looked at Samuel sternly

"You guess?"

Samuel caught himself

"WAS! I was being rude."

Talia sat silently for a moment

"I'm sorry for my hostility as well. But know that I still am watching you."

Samuel nodded and swallowed. Master Senan then began to laugh

"Like two children being made to apologies. My, my I never thought I would be doing this at my age. Ha ha" Talia and Samuel looked at Master Senan in shock. Master Senan then stood and slowed his laughter

"Young man. I wish to help you as well. I do not know why a troll would travel to your world or why they would attack a village and kidnap your sister. Your story grows stranger with each word I hear. But maybe I can lend a hand if we find your sister Emily? Was it? If you or the princess find her then I can ensure she is made to look fae."

Master Senan walked over to a cabinet and opened a drawer at his waist. He took a small purple colored stone from it and walked over to the large fire pit in his home.

"I use the hearth for cooking and this one for magic."

Master Senan then grabbed a powder from a table that sat next to the fire. It was milk white with bits of black flake in it. He threw the powder into the fire and it turned a color of blue. He then took a vile of liquid from his pocket and put a drop into the fire. The flames roared and a shade of red flowed through the blue. Master Senan then took the purple stone in hand and tossed it into the flames. It was as if the flames caught it mid fall and the stone hovered in the fire. The stone broke into two halves and Master Senan then began to chant in a language similar to Talia's song. The stones began to shake and the fire swirled around them. It was as if the stone was inhaling the flames. Samuel watched in amazement at the sight. The fire then suddenly died and the stones were now of a rainbow color. Master Senan grabbed them from the air and wrapped a string around both of them.

"Here, take these. If you find Emily give her one of these necklaces. It will make her appear fae and she will be protected from any of your father's men whom may wish to harm humans."

Samuel and Talia each took a necklace in hand. Samuel studied the necklace closely. Though it had just been in a fire the stone was not hot.

Master Senan looked to Talia and said that her and Samuel should be heading back to her father soon, before he notices they are gone. Talia nodded and hugged Master Senan

"Thank you for your help Master Senan. I hope you come to see us when this is all over."

Master Senan smiled and patted Talia on the back.

"Child you and your father and mother are my family. Your grandmother Arina and Lady Aine were my daughters. I will keep an eye on you two during your journey. If you need help, I will be there."

Samuel held out his hand and thanked Master Senan for his help and advice. Master Senan let go of Talia and shook Samuel's hand

"Young man. Protect Princess Talia with your life and she will do the same. Now be off the two of ya, I must look into something."

Talia and Samuel both walked out of Master Senna's home and closed the door. Master Senan waved and smiled as they walked out, but as soon as the door closed his smiled disappeared. He then walked back over to his fire pit and looked into the ashes. He waved his hand over the ashes of the fire and they began to swirl.

"Are you still alive?" he asked in a whisper. The ashes then formed into the figure of a woman. "It is true. I thought I felt your magic stir when I held that ring." The ashes then began to form something else next to the woman. Master Senan looked in confusion at the mound that was forming. "Good heavens. Oh, my poor dear what have you done?"

CHAPTER FIVE

As Talia and Samuel stepped out of Senan's home; Samuel looked back to the door of the house.

"That was strange, it was if he was trying to get rid of us quickly."

Talia looked to Samuel and said that Senan was an odd old man.

"I always knew the story of Lady Aine." Talia said crossing her arms and grasping her elbows. "But to see everything that had happened. It's more heart breaking then I thought it was."

Samuel turned away from the door and looked at Talia. A look of surprise was on his face as he turned

"Losing a child is always sad. The lengths some will go to protect their children are even greater than we can imagine."

Talia still holding her arms began walking down Senan's hill. Samuel huffed and followed behind her. The two mounted their horses as they made it to the bottom of the hill. The two began riding back to Charwood more slowly than before. Samuel took note of how Talia seemed to still be sad from what they had just seen. Samuel looked up at the full moon and the stars above.

"The nights sky is more beautiful here then back home." Talia raised her head and slightly turned back to Samuel whom was riding behind her.

"The night sky back home does not have the colors that yours do. Swirls of purple and pink do not dance in our skies. But the moon and her stars are the same."

Talia looked upward and began to calm herself. Samuel smiled slightly as his words seemed to help bring her peace. The ride back to Charwood was indeed slower and calmer than before, but Talia and Samuel enjoyed the night and its wonders. As the two entered back into Charwood Talia stopped her horse and looked upward.

"I thought as much!" a voice said from in front of her.

Samuel sat up on his horse and looked over Talia's shoulder. There standing before them was Captain Rollins; still in the robe he wore when he left the bath house.

"Please dismount your majesty and you as well Samuel." He said putting his hands behind his back and walking slowly towards them. Talia and Samuel stepped down from their horses.

"Where was it you two went and caused me more headache this night?" Captain Rollins asked stepping before Talia.

Talia always one with wit; looked at Captain Rollins and spoke

"We simply went for a short ride outside of town in the countryside." Captain Rollins smirked and looked over Talia's shoulder.

"And is that true men?" Talia's eyes grew and she turned to look behind her. The two horses transformed into soldiers; Talia had a dumbfounded look and sighed loudly.

"I should have recognized you replaced our horses." She said grabbing the bridge of her nose.

The two soldiers came to attention and saluted Captain Rollins by holding their fists to their chests. They then bowed to Talia and apologized for spying on her.

"Sir we traveled into the countryside to a farm house." one of the men said. Captain Rollins became confused and looked at Talia

"Whose home did you visit your majesty?" Before Talia could mutter a single syllable, a voice came from behind everyone.

"They came to my house Captain." Captain Rollins turned to find Senan standing behind them by the door of Charwood Hall.

The two soldiers dropped to one knee and bowed their heads. Captain Rollins bowed

"Master Senan. It is a privilege to see you again sir." Senan was now dressed in a red tunic with gold trim and brown trousers with black leather shoes. A far cry from the robes that Talia and Samuel had seen him in before.

"Her majesty Princess Talia came to see me and ask for my help. She wanted me to join you and her father on this quest and offer protection since you will be traveling into the Black Mountains."

Captain Rollins was taken back by Senan's statement. With a slight hesitation Captain Rollins acknowledged Senan and bowed.

"I shall see to it his Majesty King Alaois knows of your aid." with that Captain Rollins walked away from the group and into Charwood Hall.

The two soldiers stood and followed behind him. Senan turned to look at Talia and Samuel

"I must speak with you before your father comes out here. I am sorry I rushed you out of my home after showing you my memories, but I felt a presence in that ring of yours."

Talia and Samuel were confused and asked why not say anything when they were there. Senan stroked his beard and said that he had to be sure of what I felt before saying anything; less you think me mad." Before Senan could fully explain Captain Rollins returned from the hall.

"His majesty welcomes you to our expedition and regrets that he could not great you right now. He said he will see you in the morning before we depart. I must say that with your added protection no one would dare make an attempt an attack."

Senan smiled and let out a slight laugh with a ha. Senan began shuffling towards Charwood Hall and walked past Captain Rollins. Captain Rollins turned back to Talia and Samuel

"It was very clever to ask Master Senan for help Princess. Your father and I are proud of your forward thinking." With that, Captain Rollins smiled softly at Talia and followed behind Senan into Charwood Hall.

Samuel turned to Talia and asked what Senan could have wanted to tell them. Talia still looking at Captain Rollins replied

"I'm not sure. He said he felt a presence, but I don't know what he could have felt. Come, we need to get some form of sleep before morning comes." Talia and Samuel entered Charwood Hall and went to their rooms. Talia laid upon her bed and curled into a ball. "Why do I feel this way?" she said to herself.

"Why do I feel as if my heart has been pulled from my chest? I have heard the story of Lady Aine before, but..... Is it because I could actually see it? Is it

because I could see and hear her pain?" Talia looked out her room window at the moon.

Her mind went back to Samuel telling her how the night sky was much more beautiful here than in the human realm. Talia stared at the moon and stars and its silence; taking in the calming nature of it. She soon felt calm enough to fall asleep. The morning came quickly with a slight mist raising from the ground. Smoke swirled from the chimneys of Charwood and the earthen ovens making charcoal bellowed flames. Samuel sat up on his bed in Charwood Hall; rubbing his face and neck. He was still not accustomed to sleeping on such fine bedding. Back home on his farm he and his sister slept on a fleece blanket worn by time with straw underneath. These beds that he had been sleeping on were made of feathers. Samuel stood and dressed himself, putting his sword and belt on around his waist he looked to the rising sun.

"Please be alive Emily. I swear I will find you." he muttered to himself.

Samuel opened the door to his room to step out only to find Talia standing on the other side. Samuel was surprised by her standing there and asked if everything was okay.

"I wanted to thank you for helping calm me last night. I don't know why Lady Aine's story affected me so much; it never had before." Samuel was taken back by Talia's deminer and statement. To this point after finding out he was human she had been slightly callus towards him.

"I also have been thinking of what Master Senan had said and I am sorry for how I have been acting. You have only showed kindness to me and I have been listening to preconceived notions about your race."

Samuel's mouth slightly opened and his eyebrows raised.

"You're welcome and I am sorry as well. I was a bit rude last night before we left." Talia nodded and told Samuel that everyone was gathering outside in the town sqaure.

"Come on. We have to find your sister and with Master Senan helping us it should make things easier."

Talia and Samuel walked down the stairs to find the servants of Charwood Hall lined against the bottom floor walls. They bowed as Talia passed and a servant opened the front door for her and Samuel.

As they stepped outside, they found the village of Charwood was full of life. Hundreds of people filled the square and cheered as Talia came from the hall. King Alaois and Lord Cillian stood by the soldiers whom were mounted on their Pooka horses. All at attention waiting for command from their king. It was then that Senan stepped out from Charwood Hall. The people grew silent and all took a knee before him. Senan smiled and held up his hand

"Please! There is no need for such formality. Please all of you stand and enjoy your lives as free people"

The people stood and began to cheer once again. Samuel was confused at this action by the people. He leaned to his left and asked Talia why the people cheered for her and her father but kneeled for Senan. Talia explained that Senan is the last remaining founder of the kingdom and though he is powerful he has never used his magic for evil and has always sought to help.

"They cheer for my family because we maintain peace. They kneel for him because he is the greatest sorcerer to have ever lived and they respect his power." King Alaois took Senan by the hand and lord Cillian bowed.

"My dearest and oldest friend." King Alaois said with a smile "My daughter was wise to ask for your aid. With you at our side we can assure that this mission will be peaceful." Senan bowed his head

"King Alaois I was happy to be asked by Princess Talia to come on this mission."

Senan then looked to the crowd of people and raised his hand. The crowd froze in time, birds stayed motionless in the air and water in a nearby fountain stopped flowing. King Alaois looked around to see everyone frozen. Only he, Taila, Samuel and Senan were not frozen in time.

"Now I must speak to you in private." Senan said letting go of King Alaois's hand. King Alaois grew quiet and gave a concerned look towards Senan. "My old pupal is still alive."

Senan said stroking his beard. King Alaois's face grew pale and Talia asked what Senan had meant by "still alive" Senan took a few steps away from the group and rubbed his head.

"I was not quite sure but I felt her magic." Talia looked to Samuel as he grasped his hand that had the ring upon it. "I used an ash spell to see her. I don't know where she is but she is alive." King Alaois let out a deep breath from his mouth as he looked to the ground.

"How?" he asked looking back to Senan.

Senan turned to King Alaois and looked at him with a concerned look. He then looked to Talia and Samuel whom were intently listening to every word.

"Darkness comes in many forms. For some it is anger for others it is grief; for Aine it was the loss of her child." Senan took a deep breath and began to pace "I as well as you thought she had died the night she tried to use dark magic, but we were all wrong. The darkness destroyed her body yes but it planted itself into her heart. A place which if filled with darkness may never return. Now her body is back and her heart and soul have fallen to darkness. I'm coming with you to not only help young Samuel find his family but to protect you. If she has fully given in to the darkness and is hiding in the Black Mountains then I must be with you. I hope that I can save her and bring her back."

King Alaois gritted his lips and nodded. Talia asked was there any way she could help and Samuel asked the same. Master Senan nodded slightly

"If we find her, we must approach with caution. Darkness can twist the purest of hearts." King Alaois nodded and looked over to Talia.

"Talia, I want you to stay close to the guard at all times. Samuel, we will continue to look for your sister but the safety of my daughter is priority. If trouble begins then you will get her back to our castle." Samuel acknowledged King Alaois's wish with

"Yes your majesty" Senan walked back to King Alaois and patted him on his shoulder

"Alaois I am sure that things will be well. After we find Samuel's sister and get to the bottom of why they would take her; I want to stay in the mountains for a time and see if I can find her. Hopefully I can withdraw the darkness from her heart."

King Alaois replied "I hope you are right Master Senan. Now please restore please time; we must be off on our journey. We have a couple hours ride ahead of us."

Senan nodded with a final stroke of his beard and waved his hand. The people once again came alive and cheered for the group. Lord Cillian once again came alive and a smile grew more on his face.

"I wish you all well and please stop here on your way back. I shall have a better prepared feast for all of you."

King Alaois slapped both of Lord Cillian's shoulders and said that his stomach may not be able to handle it. The two laughed as friends would and King Alaois did not let the weight of Senan's concern show. Captain Rollins then rode into Charwood followed by four soldiers.

"Your Majesty, Master Senan, Lord Cillian I have come back from the mountain pass gates. The men are on standby awaiting our arrival."

King Alaois told Captain Rollins it was good he had the men awaiting them as he wanted to make it quickly through the pass.

"Those mountains are a wall in of themself." King Alaois said putting on his ridding gloves.

The group mounted their horses; as Talia sat on her horse, she looked over to see the child she had sent food to, standing in the crowd. The child mouthed the words "Thank you" to Talia. Talia smiled and bowed her head to the child. Lord Cillian looked at Senan and noticed that he did not have a horse to ride.

"Good heavens Master Senan." he said with smile "You don't intend to walk forty miles to the mountain wall and gates?"

Senan laughed at Lord Cillian's question; holding his hand high into the air above his head. A bolt of lightning struck Senan and in the flash he was gone. People gasped at the sight and looked around. King Alaois laughed and told the people of Charwood that Master Senan need never walk again for he rides the winds themself.

The people were amazed by the power that they had just witnessed. Many whispering amongst themselves that the stories of his power are true. King Alaois looked from the people to his men and ordered them to take the lead. The platoon of soldiers replied with a shout "YES SIR!" a shout that echoed throughout the village. The men began to ride in their filed line and King Alaois, Talia, and Samuel fell into the center of them. Captain Rollins rode hard past the column and made it to the front; taking the lead.

"Good luck my friends! May your journey be fruitful." Lord Cillian called out to the group as they left.

As the column left town, they entered into the forest that surrounded the town. Taking a different road of that which Talia and Samuel took the night before. The forest was calm and cool with the morning sun glimmering through the tree tops. The haze of the morning dew rose over the forest floor. The column rode for over an hour to the east; even from a distance the looming shadows of the Black Mountains towered over the land. A naturally formed wall dividing the land. The eastern lands of Dreegahnna were narrow due to this and very little farm land was there. The only thing that made the lands of the east viable for settlement was the fact the Black Mountains were rich in iron and obsidian and the eastern coast line was rich with fish and perfect for sailing. Still, that did not degrade the fact the land was ruled by the descendants of those Arina Dreegahnna had deposed. Aristocratic trolls, land baron goblins, lording dark mages all held claim over the Black Mountains and its people. Samuel was curious about this fact and asked King Alaois why had he not finished the aristocracy during the war. King Alaois had a serious look on his face and let out a deep breath through his nose.

"When my son Tomlin was killed, I wanted nothing more." He said gripping his horse's reign. "I rallied my legion and we drove the dark forces back to the eastern coast; past the Black Mountains even. But we had over stretched ourselves and my ranks had been worn thin. We surrounded the coastal port town of Vera. The last of the lords had held inside in by collapsing houses of stone and wood and making a rough wall."

"But even had we taken Vera I was still getting reports of raids on our towns. We still had enemy forts that had not yet fallen. The legions were thin and weak and the people were suffering. The aristocracy sent a messenger under a white flag. If I agreed to leave Vera and all lands around the Black Mountains; They would end the war and order all attacks on Dreegahnna to cease. It must have been five days of intense negotiations. I agreed that they may keep all land east of the mountains if they give me the mage who killed my son, all raids stop, and they free the people whom were still in chains. They agreed to hand the mage over on the condition the last of their slaves stay and to stop all raids if we gave them part of the Black Mountains and the east coast. I was reluctant to leave anyone in chains. I had seen the horrors of it in the lands we had liberated, but I was filled with vengeance and wanted to bring peace to my tired and war-torn people."

Samuel hung on every word the king said. He felt that King Alaois should have held out and freed all the slaves but he sympathized with his rage. Senan's words from before then echoed in Samuel's head.

"Darkness can consume anyone and it has many forms."

Samuel felt a small drop in his heart when the words echoed. Though King Alaois had avenged his son's death he condemned many to still suffer, however he had ended the suffering of many more. He began to think if had had been in the same situation. Would he condemn a few to suffer to save many or would he prolong the suffering of all to save a few? As Samuel thought about this dilemma the massive stone gates to the Black Mountain pass began to emerge over the tree tops. The gate consisted of four identical towers of stone; forming a box shape with stone walls connecting them. The wooden spire roof tops towered high at one hundred feet. A purple flag with a broken chain cut by a sword flew over each tower. Samuel took note of the flags as they seemed different from the ones that flew at the capitol. Samuel asked Talia why this was and she explained that the flags at the gates represented the fact that Dreegahnna was formed from slaves whom freed themselves and would fight to keep it that way.

The column arrived at the massive gates as the sun was almost half way in the sky. The cool morning air was giving way to the heat of the noon and shadows began to become thinner in size. Soldiers of the gate stood in attention in four rows deep in front of the gate. Archers stood atop of the walls and towers with their bows upright. The gates were two large doors made of logs weld together by iron; and an iron grate gate hung over the door. Ready to swing downward and be locking into place to reinforce the doors. King Alaois rode forward with Captain Rollins and inspected the soldiers guarding the gate. It was then Master Senan appeared before everyone with a flash of light.

"The way is clear and safe." Senan explained to King Alaois. "I sent word to the aristocracy to expect us and that this was a diplomatic mission. They expect us by half past noon."

King Alaois nodded and ordered the soldiers to open the gates. The massive log gates jolted and began to moan as they opened. A second set of doors opposite began to open as well and soon a narrow rocky path lay before the group. The shadows of the mountains seemed to cloak the path in darkness and a chill passed through everyone as the doors fully opened.

"It's just as grim as it was the last time we passed through." Captain Rollins said. King Alaois had a stern look and nodded

"This time we are more rested and prepared." Captain Rollins hmphed at the king's words.

"We are also fifteen years older and not as spry."

King Alaois let out a slight chuckle and a small smile came to his face. Master Senan walked up to King Alaois and said that he will be at the town of Vera shortly.

"I want to check an old fortress not far from here." King Alaois knew Senan had a mission of his own, to find Lady Aine and try to help her.

"Yes, I want to leave nothing to chance. Do what you must Master Senan."

King Alaois said. Master Senan then held up his hand and once again a bolt of lightning carried him away. The pass before them was so narrow that they would have to travel two side by side rather than four side by side. Captain Rollins took the lead and asked the King Alaois, Talia, and Samuel ride in the center for better protection. As the column narrowed into the rocky pass of the Black Mountains; the cold shade of its shadows chilled many of the group to the bone. Though Master Senan had said the troll aristocracy guaranteed no attack will happen to them; the nerves of all were high. The rocky walls of the pass were jagged and sharp. They seemed to tower high into the sky above the clouds.

"Is this really the only way through the mountains?" Samuel asked Talia.

"Yes" Talia replied "Someone could try to go over the mountains another way but it would be near imposable for there is no roads."

Though the pass was narrow it was surprisingly short via horse back. It only took the column forty minutes to come to the other side. As the column came out of the pass the grey and gloom of the mountains seemed to stay behind them. The pass rested on a small hillside that was clear of all trees; a valley of no more than three miles wide sat at its base. A massive ocean laid opposite of the mountain pass; with no adjacent shore in sight. The column of soldiers came out of the pass and filed back into normal ranks of four men side by side.

As King Alaois came out of the pass with Talia and Samuel behind him the sun glinted off of his armor. A pause came over the king as he gazed upon the valley and the distant roar of the ocean tide splashed upon the sandy shores. The sound of swords clinging and men shouting filled King Alaois's mind. Captain Rollins turned his gaze from the ocean back to the king.

"Your Majesty?" He asked slightly lowering his head.

King Alaois broke his focus and looked upward at the captain. A brief moment of silence stood between them as the king regained his surroundings.

"The last time I was here I fought with the ferocity of a hundred men. Now I stand here in the calm of hallowed ground remembering the fallen."

Captain Rollins slightly opened his mouth but fell with the loss of words as he did not know what to say. Talia heard what her father had said and rode her horse to his side. She placed her hand on his shoulder and looked at him.

"Father. You did what you had to in the moment. I miss Tomlin with all my heart and know that you brought justice to his killer. But that battle is now over and we have had peace for fifteen years since."

King Alaois placed his hand on Talia's and looked at her; taking in every word she said. "Come!" the king said taking his hand from Talia's

"We have a two-hour ride from here to the town of Vera. We must not delay."

As the column fully formed Captain Rollins asked that Talia and Samuel be placed back into the center. King Alaois began to ride ahead of the column with Captain Rollins riding beside him. Many of the soldiers were on edge as they had only vague memories from childhood or no memory at all to the violence the aristocracy's army delivered in its raid and attacks.

"Many of the men look on edge." Samuel said to Talia in a lowered voice.

"Even I am slightly on edge." Talia replied "I have never been to these lands and do not know what to expect. Only my father and Captain Rollins have been here before during the final days of the war."

The land seemed to be covered in a grey sky with very few trees. A lone dirt road stretched from the mountain pass leading to Vera. With ocean on their right and valley and mountains to their left; the column was in the open.

"I don't like being this exposed your Majesty." Captain Rollins said in a low voice.

King Alaois's eyes were shifting all around looking for the first sign of movement.

"I don't like it myself Captain, but we must press on." King Alaois slowed his horse allowing the column to pass him until he was at its center.

Soon he was riding next to Talia and Samuel and asked that they step out of the column.

"I want you two to go find Samuel's sister. You WILL take ten men with you; with the Pooka Dragoon that will give you twenty men for protection. No one will harm you while you bare my standard. At the first sign of trouble return home and raise the legions."

King Alaois then ordered ten of his men to stay with Talia and Samuel and to protect them.

"There is a nearby village that mines much of the iron from the mountains. Start there but go no further. This way you are still close enough to the pass to make a quick escape." Samuel could tell the king was on edge and asked if he thought something will go wrong. King Alaois took a deep breath and replied

"Something can always go wrong; but we have not heard the cry of the Banshee nor has the Dullahan called our names. Death is not with us this day." Talia leaned over and hugged her father. King Alaois patted her on her back and told her to be safe in the search.

"Samuel, I hope we do find your sister. Nothing would bring me peace than to eradicate this land and bring full peace to the kingdom."

Talia and Samuel took the ten men and began riding down a separate path from the one they had been on. As King Alaois watched them ride away, Captain Rollins rode next to him.

"She reminds me of the stories I heard as a child. Of your mother Queen Arina." King Alaois hmphed at Captain Rollins words.

"That's what worries me as her father but also makes me proud as king. I know she will lead this land justly on day." the king replied. "Let's try to give them time to search. I feel that what Samuel has told us is all true."

Captain Rollins than asked why King Alaois was willing to help so quickly. What if Samuel did not have any family and this was all a cleaver ploy?

"Captain" King Alaois said "Have you ever had a feeling about someone? Whether you like them or not? Have you ever thought that you can trust someone without worry?"

Captain Rollins went silent and thought. He then let out a huff and replied

"I have only had that feeling twice in my life your Majesty." King Alaois nodded and slightly smiled

"I know. He felt the same about you."

The column soon reached the town of Vera. It was far different from the last time King Alaois and Captain Rollins had last been there. New high stone wall surrounded the town. The walls had many soldiers of fairy origan wearing armor made of darkened iron. Many of them sneering at the sight of King Alaois and his men. In a soft low voice King Alaois spoke

"I wish I did not leave them nor their families in chains."

Captain Rollins replied that he did not want too as well, but we had to end the war. The column stopped at the gates of Vera which were made of pure iron.

"That is different from the last time." Captain Rollins said to King Alaois.

The gates opened with a groaning wail of iron on iron. Many of the king's men made slight faces as the noise pierced their ears. As the gates fully opened the town of Vera was reviled to the king and his men. It was a town similar to Charwood with different types of building made of wood and stone. A market of fruit, wheat, fish, and meat sat near its entrance. King Alaois and his men slowly rode into the town; Goblins who stood at three feet tall with grey and green skin walked around in fine satin clothing. A few dark mages dressed in black cloaks and eyes of dark purple glared at King Alaois and his men. Very few leprechauns were in Vera but all that were either were shining the boots of goblins and mages or were toiling in shops making shoes for them. It was than on the edge of the market the truth that had haunted the king for years greeted him. Standing on a wooden stage was a troll in fine fleece of red and brown selling slaves.

Fairy folk of different shade and heugh, short and tall, young and old were being sold to the highest bidders. Many of King Alaois's men were deeply disturbed by the sight of the auction. The slaves were in brown burlap with a rope on the waist line. Some had old leather shoes that barely held together and others had none. The troll stood almost eight foot in height; an average height for their kind. In a deep graveled voice, he shouted to the crowd.

"We have here a child of seven winters! She is young and strong not yet whipped! She will make a good scullery maid or chamber maid! When she is older, she will make many more, good healthy slaves! Who will give me one hundred gold coins!"

One of the soldiers from the guard grew angry and started to break formation. Captain Rollins saw this and rode to the soldier.

"I know!" he said to the soldier in a soft shout "It's sick and vial but we can do nothing. This is a mission of peace."

The soldier bit his bottom lip to a point of blood coming out. He looked up at the child and noticed the troll looking at him and slightly smiling. The soldier used all of his will power to look away and fall back into rank. He was not alone in his feeling as many of the king's men were sickened by the sight. King Alaois had a look of worry and regret upon his face as it was his choice that allowed this to continue. A large manner sat in the towns center surrounded by stone watch towers. A large double wooden door sat at the center of the manners face with arched windows on both sides. The doors opened and an older Troll with oily grey hair slicked back to the base of his neck walked out. He wore a long blue robe with a brown vest underneath. Burgandy colored trousers with fringed bottoms met nicely shined black boots with golden buckles. His skin was grey with a large nose and ears full of grey hair.

"Welcome King Alaois Dreegahnna" he said in a baritone like voice.

King Alaois and his men stopped in front of the manner.

"Lord McHarris, I thank you for the time you have granted us." King Alaois said as he dismounted his horse. Lord McHarris stepped forward and placed his hands in two small pockets.

"I believe the last time I saw this many of your men was when you near ended my life." McHarris said smugly.

Many of the soldiers fought to hold their tongs as their king was insulted. Lord McHarris looked over to Captain Rollins.

"I believe that you were here as well. Not much younger than you are now."

King Alaois raised an eyebrow to Lord McHarris's words. Thinking that he should calm the mood King Alaois replied.

"But peace was all that I was fighting for; and peace was achieved between the two of us." Lord McHarris slightly tilted his head and replied.

"With you owning lands that my ancestors called home and I forced to live in my families former summer home. Even the number of slaves that I and the other lords have was decreased by you and your men. However, through proper breeding we are raising that number have used the trading ports on the edge of this town to build our finances back. What...brings...you...here... your majesty?"

Captain Rollins gripped the hilt of his sword and stared at Lord McHarris. King Alaois's nerves were high and he thought his of his carefully.

"I simply wish to visit this land and maybe mend the wounds between us. Both our children shall one day take over rule of our lands and we should try to ease the tension between our two nations."

Lord McHarris ran his tong across his bottom teeth and let out a low hum.

"Then what do you have in mind to ease tensions?" He said in his baritone voice.

King Alaois cleared his throat and began a small list of suggestions.

"Trading iron for some of our crops, charcoal to use in your forges."

Lord McHarris held up his large wrinkled hand to the king. Many of the soldiers grew angrier at the disrespect Lord McHarris was showing to their king and the son of the woman whom had freed their families from the fate they had passed in the market.

"These are small agreements that we have already with other kingdoms. Thus, how we have been able to build our walls and arm our soldiers." Lord McHarris said lowering his hand back to his vest pocket.

While the conversation between Lord McHarris and King Alaois was happening. Talia, Samuel, and their small detachment of soldiers arrived at a small mining town at the base of the black mountains. The town had no name and was dingy, muddy, and smelled of animal dung. Many hogs and chickens sat in pens; sickly in looks and unfit to even slaughter. Many of the soldier covered their noses to the smell and Talia held her hand over his mouth.

"The smell is ghastly." She said holding back the urge to vomit.

Samuel whom was accustomed to farming was not put off by the smell but was put off by the sickened animals.

"These animals are beyond sick and weak." He said looking down from his horse as they rode by. "If one was to eat their meat or eggs, they would be sick themselves. One is better to eat dirt then eat these animals."

It was then the group stopped and gazed upon the people of the town. All of them were covered in filth and looked like walking skeletons.

"Ghouls" one of the soldiers said.

Talia shook her head and replied "No. They are living."

Many of the people seemed to toil by sharpening picks and shovels. All the elderly either sat sewing holes in clothes or cooking what little food they had. It was then that a wagon pulled into town; a small goblin climbed down from the wagons seat and opened the back of it.

"Out! All of you out!" he shouted in a scratching voice.

The goblin then took a stick from his belt and began beating the side of the wagon. Many small children jumped out of the back of the wagon. Some crying others to afraid to even make a sound. A troll stepped out from a small house smoking a long neck pipe; a dark mage at his side. With a puff of smoke leaving his mouth he told the children that they now belong to him and will be put to work in the iron mines. This sent a bolt of anger through Talia and the soldiers. But Samuel was distracted by the sight of these creatures. Was it one of these creatures that took his sister Emily?

He had to find her and take her home from this place. One of the soldiers rode next to Talia griping his sword hilt.

"Your Majesty" the soldier said glaring at the sight "Give us the word and we will set them free."

Talia remembering her father wanted to keep this peaceful ordered the soldiers to stand down. It was then the Pooka Dragoon horse looked up to Talia.

"Please your Majesty. If we transform you will have twenty of us to command and fight at your side. We cannot leave these children here to suffer like this."

Talia gripped her reigns and looked on to the sight. It was then her eyes turned to the dark mage whom was staring back to her. His purple eyes seemed to pierce Talia to her soul.

"We can't do anything." Talia said swiftly "We have our mission for now but I swear we will return one day."

The dark mage seemed to understand what Talia was saying from so far away and smiled. A rage filled Talia but she managed to keep her cool when suddenly Samuel took Talia's hand. Talia looked down at her hand then back to Samuel.

"Don't give him the satisfaction." Samuel said through the side of his mouth; looking at the dark mage.

The soldier that had asked to save the children then looked over and saw a woman in a house. She was holding a worn hole riddled drape up waving for the soldier to come to her.

The soldier turned and told Talia that someone was trying to get their attention. Talia turned her head slightly looking over the soldier's shoulder to the woman in the window. Samuel then leaned over to Talia and told her they should split up in order to cover more ground. Talia nodded and turned to the soldiers behind her and shouted

"Go in groups of two! We are guests here so keep your blades sheathed!"

The soldiers responded in a softer yes than what they had given back in Charwood. Talia then looked to Samuel.

"We need to ask around and find your sister before the men do. I also want to know why the woman in that house is trying to get our attention." Samuel nodded and dismounted his horse; Talia followed suit and dismounted as well.

The two tied their horses to a hitching post next to a building. A troll came out of the build and looked at Talia and Samuel.

"I know who are your HIGHNESS." the troll said in a disgusted tone. "If you wish to tie your horses to my building you will pay a fee."

Talia became angered by the troll's tone but held out a small bag of coins none the less. The troll opened the bag and sifted through with his large fingers.

"This will give you half hour use." The troll then walked back into the building and slammed the door.

Talia glared at the door when Samuel spoke. "Then let's not give him reason to charge us more."

Talia nodded and began looking around the town slowly making their way to the house where the woman had been signaling. It was a rundown house more akin to a shanty then a suitable home. Talia and Samuel looked around to make sure no one was looking and then proceeded to knock on the door. The door slowly cracked open and the woman whom had been signaling peeked out from behind the door.

"Quickly come in." she said opening the door swiftly.

Talia and Samuel stepped through and the woman looked around and closed the door. The woman was dressed in what appeared to be a white dress the stopped at her ankles. The dress was worn, dirty, and had many patches of different cloth holding it together. A small rope was tied around her waist which was thin and starved. Her face was gaunt like that of a corpse and her hair thin and patchy with bald spots. Talia and Samuel were amazed by the woman appearance.

"It sickens me to see all of you in this shape." Talia said holding back a tear.

Samuel nodded at Talia's statement and asked if the woman was in need of help. The woman apologized for her appearance and brushed herself off. She then bowed to Talia and fell to her knees. Talia reached forward to catch her and Samuel jolted his arm out to help as well. Talia grabbed the woman by her upper arms close to the shoulders. The woman with tears in her eyes looked up to Talia.

"Your Majesty. I have no money nor land to give, but I ask that you take my child with you when you leave. I hide her birth from my lord and do not want her to live in chains as I do."

Talia looked at the woman with compassion and Samuel and could feel the sadness of the room come over him. Talia stumbled over her words; almost at a loss for what to say. Talia gained her composure

"I will take your child from this land, but I must ask one thing."

The woman was overjoyed and smiled widely showing that some of her teeth were gone and others had rot.

"You need only name it your Majesty." Talia stood and looked to Samuel "I think you may need to show her."

Samuel thought and kneeled down to the woman; he then removed his ring reveling his human form. The woman was shocked and her mouth shuttered.

"I've never seen your kind mortal. I've only heard the stories of my ancestors about your kind."

Samuel apologized for deceiving her but he had to do so to save someone important to him. The woman swallowed and looked to Talia

"If the princess trusts you then so do I." Samuel smiled and put his ring back on.

"I am searching for my sister Emily. She was brought to this realm by a troll from what I have been told. She has no magic to hide her and is human in form. Have you seen or heard anything?" he asked looking at the woman.

The woman looked down; her eyes looking all over as she thought.

"I may have sir. I heard my lord speaking at a dinner last night. He, spoke of a spell that required the blood of a virgin human girl. I know not what spell uses such a thing for it is a rare commodity in this realm."

Samuel looked back to Talia and then back to the woman.

"Did your lord say anything else?"

The woman shook her head and held up her finger.

"The mage my lord was speaking to did though. He, spoke of an old fortress in the mountains. I am sorry sir but that is all I know."

Samuel took the woman by her hands and patted them.

"That is more than enough. I shall help Princess Talia take your child from this land and see she is given a home."

The woman hugged Samuel and staggered to her feet. She then hugged Talia saying "Thank you" over and over. The women then realized who she was hugging and let go.

"I am deeply sorry your Majesty." Talia smiled and hugged the woman back.

"Fetch your child and we will ensure her safety." Talia said to the woman with care in her voice.

The woman held back tears and said nothing as Talia let go of her. The woman went into another room separated only by a thin and torn pinkish/red rag acting as a curtain. Samuel looked to Talia

"It will be difficult to get a child out of this town without being seen."

Talia nodded and said that they will form the soldiers in deep ranks with the child at center.

"I want to make it to the fortress quickly. If Emily is there then I have to help her."

Samuel said with slight urgency. Talia slightly nodded and bit her lip.

"Master Senan was going to that same fortress. There is only one fortress in the mountains. She is more protected by him then us and he knows of your situation. We have to help this child get to the kingdom." Talia said crossing her arms.

It was then the woman returned from behind the curtain; an infant wrapped in a tan rag in her arms. The child couldn't have been more than a month old but was so malnourished that it appeared very small.

"This is my daughter Aisling. I fear if she does not get better care soon, she will not survive." The woman said looking happily at her child.

With tears in her eyes, she handed the baby to Talia whom took her into her breast.

"Her heart is weak and she is starved." Talia said looking concerned at the child. "I will see she is given a home and cared for with much love."

The woman began to cry and placed her hand on the baby's head. She then said for them to take care and be well.

"I hope you find your family mortal; they are all some of us have in this world."

Samuel slowly nodded and could only think that Emily would want him to see this child safe before her. She had always wanted to be a mother he thought. Talia asked Samuel to open the house door and make sure no one was watching. Samuel turned and opened the door slowly peering out into the street. Many slaves toiled about their day and a few of the soldiers had returned to the side of Talia and Samuel's horses. Samuel fully leaned out and looked to where the dark mage and troll had been watching before. They had gone from the location and it was safe to leave. Samuel turned and gave an assuring nod to Talia that it was clear. Talia grabbed the woman with one arm and hugged her again.

"If ever you can free yourself from this land, seek my castle out. Your daughter will be waiting for you." She said holding the woman.

As this was happening Master Senan was investigating the fortress. It was a looming castle perched high on the mountain side overlooking the Kingdom of Dreegahnna. In it day it was packed with soldiers whom stood watch over the land. Now it sat in disrepair with one of the two towers collapsed. A large iron gate that once stood strongly laid rusting in the mud; half on its hinge. Spider webs littered its windows and corners with the smell of rotting wood emanating from inside. Master Senan looked all around the castle careful of each step for many wooden floors had now given way to rot.

"Your presence has led me here, but why?" He said stroking his beard.

He then made his way to the roof of the fortress. Up a winding stone staircase in one of the towers he climbed. A wooden door still sat atop of the stairs. It took a few shoves from Master Senan to make the door budge but soon it gave way. When the door opened, he saw her; sitting on the edge of the fortress in a milk white shirt tucked into brown trousers with brown leather boots was Aine. She sat gazing out over the land of Dreegahnna with one leg bent and the other hanging over the fortress edge. Master Senan was taken back by her sitting there for he as well as everyone thought she had died long ago. Though Master Senan had seen her in his vison alive; to see her in the flesh gave his heart great joy and relief.

"My child." Master Senan said slowly "I thought you gone from this world long ago."

Aine said nothing and slightly turned her head to him. She then stood and turned to face Master Senan. It was then Master Senan's heart sank as he saw Aine's once green eyes now glowed with purple.

"Oh, my child" he said shaking his head "I knew you had been taken by the darkness but did not know you had fully given in to it." Aine slowly looked down to the ground.

"I wanted my child back Master." She said in a low voice "I was willing to do what it took." Aine then looked back to Master Senan "I was told the secrets of all that is the night my tower exploded. Alister's mind was too fragile to comprehend what I was showed. I did not wish him harm." Master Senan grabbed his beard and placed his other hands thumb in his belt.

"Child, I warned you of the dark magic of this world. But I know you still have good in you. Please come home with me and together we can cure it of your soul." he said with hope and concern in his voice.

Aine looked at her hand and slowly back to Master Senan.

"I want nothing more than to go home; to the land that Arina and I fought so hard to create."

Master Senan told Aine that she still can and had nothing to fear. He then held out his hand and asked her once again to return with him.

"I would Master, but I made a deal that night in my tower. One that I must uphold if I'm to ever see my child again." Aine said clutching her hand into a fist as a single tear fell from her eye.

Master Senan slightly took in his arm and with concern on his face asked.

"The Banshee as well as the Dullahan told you that a spirit may not return once it has crossed. What deal could you have made and with whom?"

Back in the town of Vera, King Alaois and his men still stood outside speaking to Lord McHarris.

"Well," King Alaois said grasping his hands together at his waist "I think the terms are a bit steep, but I think we can accommodate them."

Lord McHarris took out a small pipe and stuffed it with a strange weed that smelled of sulfur and roses. He stuffed it into his pipe and lit it. As smoke left his mouth, he looked at King Alaois and his men.

"Before you go your Majesty. I wish to give you a gift." Lord McHarris said puffing on his pipe.

King Alaois asked what it was that he could have as a gift? Captain Rollins as well as the soldiers felt uneasy and began gripping their swords. Ready to fight whatever threat the trolls had for them. Taking in a deep inhale of his pipe Lord Mcharris turned to the door of his home and opened it. A dark mage stepped out of the home along with a slave pushing a table on wheels. The table had a sheet that was moving and flinching. King Alaois grew afraid of the sight and Captain Rollins gripped his sword hilt tightly.

"Tell me your Majesty; have you ever seen a Banshee that cannot wail?" Lord McHarris said as he let out a great cloud of smoke.

The dark mage grabbed the sheet and pulled it from the table. There tied to the table was a thin pale woman dressed all in white. Her mouth was bound with rags so she could not speak. Her eyes darted wildly all around until she saw King Alaois. Her gaze fixated on the king and pierced his soul.

"It hurts them to not be able to wail." Lord McHarris said taking in another puff "I have kept her for three days and she gave my men quite a fight just capturing her. But we managed to gag her and strap her to this table awaiting the right time to allow her to scream."

Captain Rollins sensing the danger told his men to form ranks and protect the king.

The soldiers dismounted and drew their swords; the Pooka Dragoons transformed and drew the swords from they had strapped to their bellies. They surrounded Lord McHarris and his dark mage; blades pointing to them. Lord McHarris smiled as inhaled a deep puff; his gaze fixed on Captain Rollins. Captain Rollins Grabbed King Alaois and told him to mount his horse and run. Lord McHarris turned his gaze to the dark mage and nodded. The mage smiled and ripped the gag from the Banshee's mouth. She let out a deafening wail that pierced the sky itself. The soldier fell to the ground holding their ears; seeing his chance Lord McHarris ran into his home and ordered the dark mage to deal with them all.

King Alaois was frozen with fear as the moment the banshee stopped screaming a thunderous voice came across an icy wind.

"KING ALAOIS DREEGAHNNA!"

It was then the sound of horse hooves thundered across the sky. King Alaois looked to the sky to see the clouds swirling above him. Lightning struck all around and the clouds soon opened. A horse as black as coal with no head pulled a carriage of black. A driver sat behind the horse cracking a whip made of a spine. The driver wore all black clothing and his head sat on the bench next to him. Its skin as pale as parchment with eyes that seemed to dart all around. As King Alaois looked on in terror and his men still holding their ears from the banshee's wail. The dark mage drew a dagger and ran it into the king's chest piercing his heart. King Alaois's face contorted into one of pain as the blade sunk deep into his chest. It was then that the dark carriage landed and its door opened. As King Alaois fell his spirit seemed to leave his body. A bloody wound over his heart he looked at the carriage. The driver grabbed his head and once again the head spoke in a thunderous voice.

"PLEASE STEP IN YOUR MAJESTY"

One of the soldiers whom had gained his composure looked up at the carriage. The headless driver's eyes looked at the soldier and with a mighty snap of his whip; blinded the young man. The solider fell screaming in pain holding his eyes. Captain Rollins looking to the soldier shouted

"DON'T LOOK AT THE DULLAHAN!"

Many of the soldiers did though; many out of fear. The Dullahan produced a small wooden bucket and swung it as one would to empty it. A shower of blood covered the men whom were looking. No sooner had the blood fell on them and the dark mages thrust forth his hands. Purple lightning seemed to shoot from his fingers into the soldiers all of them whom the blood had covered falling dead to the ground.

"RETREAT! FIND PRINCESS TALIA!" Captain Rollins shouted to the remaining men.

Captain Rollins then grabbed a hand full of dirt from the street and threw it into the eyes of the dark mage. He then grabbed the soldier whom had been struck blind and threw him over his shoulders. The men fled the city of Vera so quickly that the city guards were not able to stop them. King Alaois's spirit stood silently looking into the carriage.

"Am I at peace?" he asked in a soft voice.

"YOU ARE." replied the Dullahan.

King Alaois began walking to the carriage and as he drew near to its door a wave of calm came over him. He stepped into the carriage and the door closed behind him. Once inside the Dullahan cracked his whip and the headless horse began pulling the carriage. As the carriage moved it began to rise into the sky and the clouds opened up revealing bright light similar to the sun.

Back at the mining town; Talia and Samuel mounted their horses and ordered the soldiers to surround them and make sure no one could see what she had in her arms. As Talia gave this order the wail of the banshee came across the wind. Talia's blood ran cold as many of the soldiers in their group. Samuel had never heard such a wail and asked what it was. Talia could barely speak when one the soldiers answered.

"Tis the wail of the Banshee. Someone is fated to die this day."

Talia's mind raced to her father when her fears were suddenly confirmed as the cry of the Dullahan came across the wind. Talia let out a terrified shriek and cried

"PAPA!" tears flowed from her eyes as she clutched the baby in her arms.

One of the soldiers said that they needed to get Talia to safety and they should leave quickly. Talia in a moment of hysterics shouted

"Not without my father!"

The soldiers looked with worry at Talia. "Your Majesty" one of them said "I'm sorry. But the king's name has been called. He is gone."

Talia cried and tucked her head into the baby; Samuel reached over and patted her on the back. Talia looked up at Samuel.

"We need to move now. We get you and that child to safety and I will return to help Master Senan find my sister." he said still resting his hand on her back.

Talia looked down to the baby whom was sound asleep. Gritting her teeth and saying nothing she nodded. Samuel turned to the soldiers.

"I know I have no command over you, but we must leave now."

The soldiers acknowledged Samuel and surrounded him and Talia. The began riding out of the town; everyone on alert. Back at the fortress Master Senan had no sooner asked his question to Aine when the wail of the Banshee reached them. Master Senan turned to look behind him in the direction of the wail. He then looked back to Aine "What have you done?" he asked in fear. It was then the Dullahan's voice rang out across the mountains. Aine with sadness and regret in her voice "I'm sorry Master. I had no choice. It is the only way and he is the only one who showed me how to defy death."

Master Senan grew horrified and held his hand to the sky. Lightning struck and he was transported to Vera. As he arrived the Dullahan's coach was flying into the sky and Captain Rollins and his men were fleeing town. Master Senan looked at the dead all around and found King Alaois laying in a pool of blood on the ground; the dagger still protruding from his chest. Master Senan fell to his knees grabbing the king's head and lifting it.

"Oh, my boy." he said with sadness in his heart.

The dark mage then stood managing to rid the dirt from his eyes. He looked at Master Senan and with a wicked smile.

"Your bastard king has died like wretch he is. A mongrel born of a slave whore whom should have been reined in by her masters long ago."

Master Senan slowly raised his head and his eyes began to glow bright blue. The dark mage still smiling thrusted forth his hand to strike Master Senan with the purple lighting that fell the soldiers. Master Senan though old moved at a great speed and with a wave of his hand moved the dark mages arm to one side; causing him to miss. The dark mage was shocked by the old wizard's speed and replaced his smile with a look of shock. Master Senan then flicked his hand as to say go away. A shock wave emanated from his hand and the dark mage was sent flying into a building wall; breaking his skull upon impact. Master Senan then held up his hand and lighting took him, the king's body and the bodies of the fallen soldiers away. Talia and Samuel rode hard to the Mountain Pass with the group of soldiers. Not stopping in the slightest for any reason. As they reached the pass the soldiers told Talia and Samuel to go first and they will follow; guarding the rear.

Though the pass was narrow the group rode fast back to the gates. As soon as they arrived at the gates lighting thundered across the sky and Master Senan appeared with the king's body in his arms and all the fallen soldiers around him. Upon seeing her father's body in Master Senan's arms Talia asked Samuel to hold the baby. No sooner had Samuel taken the child and Talia had dismounted her horse and ran to her father. Master Senan laid the king's body on the ground and Talia kneeled beside him crying.

"Pappa! I'm sorry pappa. Please don't leave me. Please, please, please come back."

Many of the soldiers could not hold back their tears as King Alaois had fought to keep them and their families free during the war. Some took their helmets off and hid their faces others gritted their teeth as tears fell from their eyes.

Samuel's heart grew heavy as he felt all of this was his fault. Had he not asked for them to help him find Emily King Alaois would still be alive. It was then Master Senan looked up to Samuel.

"Strike the thought from your mind Samuel." he said with his eyes still glowing "Twas not your fault that the king fell this day. No, it was all a trap that we were destined to meet. I fear a new war now sits at our doors and we must meet it."

Master Senan turned to the soldiers "Men you have your duty. Send word across the land that war has once again come to us all and your king has given his life to see your freedom sustained. Rally more men to this gate and make it a fortress." It was then Talia managed to pull herself together and asked what master Senan was going to do. Master Senan looked down at Talia and in a firm voice replied "I must go and face my daughter."

He then held up his hand and lighting carried him away. Samuel dismounted his horse and walked over to Talia; still cradling the child in arm.

"Talia I'm sorry for all this." Samuel said with heaviness in his voice.

Talia shook her head and wiped her eyes.

"As Master Senan said it is not your fault Samuel. The trolls planned this from the start and used your sister to lure us into their lands so they can strike."

Talia stood still wiping her eyes and asked the soldiers to carry her father back to the capital. She then looked around at all the fallen soldiers and said for them to be buried with full honors and any personal affects to be returned to their families. The soldiers cleared their throats and wiped their eyes. With their fists balled and striking their chests they shouted "Yes your Majesty!"

CHAPTER SIX

As lightning roared across the sky with Master Senan, his thoughts were heavy. He soon landed back at the old mountain fortress.

"Aine what have you done?" He asked walking hurriedly towards her.

Master Senan grabbed her and turned her to face him. Her eyes were full of tears and she was trying desperately to hold them back. Master Senan's face became filled with concern.

"My dear child, Arina's son Alaois has been killed. Please tell me what deal you made and whom dares to say death can be defied?"

Lady Aine took Master Senan's hands from her shoulders.

"Master I am sorry. I followed the instructions that the dark mage gave me in that tavern. The room filled with a blinding green light and images of beasts swirled around Allister and I. It was then that King Balor appeared in the room."

As soon as Aine muttered the name, Master Senan grew pale.

"The Dark King?!" Master Senan said with fear in his eyes.

Aine nodded and wiped her eyes. She then looked at Master Senan.

"As soon as he spoke in ancient Gaelic, Allister's mind snapped and I had to make him pass out to save him from dying of fear."

Master Senan stepped slightly back and listened with fear shaking him to his soul.

"King Balor told me that a soul could be brought back from the afterlife with a certain spell. He told me half the spell but said that I must help him with something before he would speak the rest. The eye on his crown then opened and the light grew in the room. So much so I had to shield my eyes, but it was too much and I passed out. When I came to, I was in a land of darkness and fog. King Balor stood over me with his hand held out. As I took it, I felt all the light magic in me leave and be replaced with darkness."

Master Senan shook his head slowly at what he was hearing.

"Child, I know you are heartbroken over your son's death. Even I am broken over it. But to make a deal with the Dark King Balor. What in heavens name did he ask you to do and why was a human needed?"

Aine took a deep breath and calmed herself.

"He asked me to put him back on the throne of the land. I said I would do it after Arina had left this world and not a moment sooner. He agreed to my terms and we spent years planning all of this. The last war was a distraction so we could gather the materials necessary to place him back on the throne. And we needed the blood of a human who was pure."

As Aine spoke, a tear fell from Master Senan's eye.

"My child, that monster will not give you a way to bring your son back. He will only give you a way to destroy yourself. Please come home with me and we will purge the darkness from your body and soul. I will need your help to find and stop any vile plans he has." Master Senan said holding out his hand.

Aine looked to the ground and shook her head.

"I have to take the risk Master." she said sniffling through her nose. "And I regret that Alaois and his son died for all this. But I can't let you stop this now. Not when I am so close to having my son back in my arms."

Master Senan's hand fell and his lips shuttered "Child, the darkness of grief has clouded your heart and that monster has fanned its flames. Please do not follow his lies." Master Senan paused and then asked. "I must know why a human girl was taken? What magic requires her and where is she?"

Aine was confused by her master's request. "What does it matter for a human?"

Master Senan stepped forward and replied "Her brother and only family has come here to find her. He actually had help from Magdalen and Allister."

Aine, though confused, relented and said "If a human is willing to risk death for his family, I will tell you. King Balor is finished with her anyway. She is in a small village to the south of here. There is an old stronghold from the war at the base of the mountains."

Upon hearing this master Senan pulled a small wooden bird from his pocket and whispered to it. The bird then came to life and flew from his hand.Aine watched the bird fly away with a smile.

"You still enjoy that old trick, don't you?" Master Senan asked.

Aine smiled and tucked her hair behind her ear "You always made me laugh as a little girl with that trick. I never did thank you for taking me in when I was a child."

Master Senan smiled "Child I took you in because you needed help controlling you power. I took you in because everyone was afraid of you for what happened to your home. I took you in because it was the right thing to do. Now please come home with me and do the right thing."

Aine shook her head and said that she can't, she had to see this through. Aine then wiped a tear from her eye and thrusted her hand forward. A flash of purple lightning burst forth towards Master Senan. Master Senan crossed his arms in front of his face and a blue shield of light formed around him. The lightning was so powerful Master Senan was pushed back across the roof of the old fort. As the blast roared around him Master Senan shouted.

"Please do not make me do this! I am not the young waring mage I was when I took you girls in. But I will not hold back if you continue. Please don't fight me, come home!" He said one final time.

Aine shook her head again and replied with a no.

"I have to do this!" She then began to float in the air.

Her eyes filled with purple light and lightning began to emanate from her hands. Master Senan watched as she lifted from the fortress roof with the wailing winds.

"Very well my beloved daughter." he said with heartbreak in his voice and a tear falling from his eye.

It was then Master Senan produced a small crystal. It was worn and cracked in appearance; due to many years of holding.

"I will fight you, if it is to save you from that monster." he said gripping the crystal in hand.

He then raised it high above his head and smashed it on the stone roof of the fortress. It was at the moment of impact a great blinding blue light darted from the crystal into Master Senan. His tunic burst into flames and burned from his body; leaving only his trousers and shoes. It was then that his spine straitened and the old feeble body he had had become young; his muscles large and defined. His beard shortened to his chest and his eyes glowed bright blue with light. It was as if the sands of time had reversed and he had regained his youthful vitality. Upon seeing this, Aine used both her hands to fire a blast of flames at Master Senan. Using only one hand, a mere flick of his wrist, Master Senan stopped Aine's blast. When Aine beheld the sight, her eyes widened and she looked down in surprise at her master. Master Senan looked up at Aine, eyes hardened with resolve, he drew back his other arm as to throw something. His hand gripped into a fist as a ball of blue flame formed in his palm. With a mighty thrust forward, a shockwave rattled the mountains. The fortress below them was instantly destroyed by the force and a thunderous roar echoed for miles.

Aine held her arms as Master Senan had done before and a transparent shield of purple light formed around her. But it was no match for the old mage and his power, her shield was shattered as she was flung far into the forest below the mountains. Master Senan then began to rise in the air and fly forward, sending forth another shockwave barreling towards her at the speed of light. Aine had hit dozens of trees as she fell into the forest, trailing a path of destruction. A large crater lay under her and she held her stomach, winded from the blast. She rolled slightly to her side and looked up to see Master Senan hovering over her. "End this now Aine, I do not want to fight you! You are forcing me to do something I do not wish to do!" Master Senan shouted as he hovered. Aine looked all around and then back to Master Senan. She then gritted her teeth and smacked the dirt below her with both arms extended.

Two large columns of dirt arose from both her sides and curved in towards Master Senan. Master Senan held out both of his arms with his hands up right. The columns halted right as his hands touched them. Aine then used the heel of her foot and smacked the ground again. Another column of dirt burst forward towards Master Senan from behind him.

Right as he looked over his shoulder, he was struck in the stomach by a large tree.

Aine had grabbed a small twig that lay next to her and caused it to grow into a massive tree. The air left Master Senan's body and his mouth went agape. As Master Senan lurched forward slightly, Aine flew to her feet and threw a blast of flames into Master Senan's face. Master Senan was sent flying into the ground creating another crater. As Aine flew over Master Senan, purple lightning and flames swirled around her. "Give up Master! I have won this fight!" she said with confidence in her voice. Master Senan rubbed the back of his neck and looked to Aine.

"Child didn't I teach you better?" It was then the clouds above them gathered and darkened. Aine looked up right as a massive bolt of lightning struck, her.

Aine screamed as her body was electrified. Master Senan stood to his feet and looked up. As the lightning stopped Aine still hovered in the air. It was then small stones around Master Senan's feet began to rise from the ground. Master Senan looked down at them preparing himself for what was to come. Aine raise her head gritting her teeth. Purple light emanated from her eyes and she looked angerly at Master Senan. Aine then let out a shout that seemed to shake the earth itself. All stones and rocks nearby began to swirl around Master Senan. The tones began to strike Master Senan from all directions. The sound of which seemed to create thunder. As Master Senan held his arms to his face to protect himself he stamped his foot into the ground. A cocoon of dirt formed around him shielding him from Aines attack. Aine upon seeing this drew her hand back and a ball of flame and lightning formed in it. She then thrusted her hand forward and a column of flames and lighting struck Master Senan's cocoon. The cocoon was instantly destroyed reveling Master Senan was not inside. Aine became confused and a look of surprise came over her face.

It was then a large tornado formed behind her in the sky. Its winds roared and shook the forest below. Lightning danced in the clouds above it and what seemed like flames began to pour from its center and were pulled into the spiraling winds of the tornado. Aine look in shock at the sight.

Thinking quickly, she held her hand out and another twig flew from the ground to her hand. It wrapped itself around her arm and soon her body. Forming a large pod of wood around her. The tornado's base arched from the sky and sucked Aine's wooden pod into it. Rocks, lightning, and flames bombarded Aine's wooden pod. The heat from which made Aine sweat profusely; cracks formed on Aines pod and the orange light of flames began to peer through. Before Aine could fully react, her wooden pod exploded and the full force of the tornado's fury let forth a barrage upon her body. Rocks, lightning, flames, and blistering wind battered her. Aine was flung far into a nearby mountain side. Its top exploding with such great force the mountain seemed to have been flattened. The tornado then died away and Master Senan hovered high in the sky, looking down at where Aine had landed.

He then slowly floated down to the now destroyed mountain and found her laying in a creator filled with rocks.

"My dear child I am so sorry." Master Senan said flying closer "I begged you not to fight me yet you felt it necessary. I will take you home now and purge that darkness from your soul. King Balor will not twist you to his will anymore."

Right as Master Senan said this Aine opened her eyes. With a speed unmatched she sat up and threw a small stone at Master Senan. The stone formed into a sharp point as it flew through the air and pierced Master Senan's chest. The stone exploded from his back with a spray of blood. Master Senan held his hand to his chest in shock. He looked down at his hand to find it covered in blood. It was then that a dark shadow cast over him. Master Senan looked up to see Aine flying high above him, her arms stretched above her head. A large mountain hovered above Aine as she looked at Master Senan in anger. Master Senan looked briefly in surprise and then smiled.

"I am so proud of the woman you have become. The light will save you one day, do not fight it."

Aine was taken back by Master Senan's words. As his smile grew Aine became filled with rage and she hurled the mountain down upon Master Senan. The mountain came down with a mighty crash on top of Master Senan. As soon as the mountain hit the ground Aine began to grow faint.

It took all her power and strength to fight her former master and she was weak from the battering of his tornado. Aine could not remain awake and she began to lose her battle with consciousness. She then slumped over and fell to the earth below. Hitting a few trees as she fell like a rag doll to the ground. As she hit the ground Aine briefly opened her eyes and looked at the tree tops that she had just fell through. Small rays of light began to pierce through the clouds and the shadow of a carriage began to come down from the light. Aine could not fight to stay awake anymore and closed her eyes. The thunderous roar from the battle between Master Senan and Lady Aine could be heard for miles. Back at the Black Mountain Pass Talia and Samuel could hear the battle rage.

"Is that a storm?" Samuel asked while still holding the baby.

Talia helped three soldiers lift her father's body and place it on a flat cart pulled by a horse.

"It sounds as if Master Senan is in a fight." Talia said as she let go of her father's body.

Talia wiped tears from her eyes as a soldier placed a blanket from the gate house over him.

With a sniff from her nose Talia continued "How could we have fallen into this trap so easily?"

Samuel walked over to Talia and placed his hand on her shoulder. Talia seemed unphased by Samuel's action, her gaze fixed on her father's body.

"I know how you feel Talia." Samuel said with care in his voice "I lost my mother when I was young and my father only a few short years ago. I…"

But before Samuel could finish Talia placed her hand on Samuel's. "Please don't say anymore Samuel."

Samuel understanding Talia's feelings slowly pulled his hand from her shoulder. Trying to think of a way to ease her mind Samuel looked to the baby curled in his arms.

"It was good of you to take this child from that horrid place." he said looking at the babe.

Talia turned and looked at Samuel, their eyes meeting as she did so. "I think this child will grow up happy and healthy as she should."

Talia took comfort in Samuel's words and looking at the resting child in his arms brought peace to her mind. The moment was soon interrupted by the sound of hooves beating on the ground rapidly. The soldiers at the gate sprang to action and formed a shield wall at the mountain pass. Their swords pointed to the sound as they readied themselves for battle. Talia gripped her sword ready to draw it at a moment's notice. It was then the source of the sound was seen. Captain Rollins and two other men on horseback burst through the pass. Their horses stopping to rear at the sight of the soldier's blades.

"Lower your blades!" He shouted to the men.

Before any of the men could react to his command Talia hurriedly pushed her way through the soldier's line and walked up to Captain Rollins. The captain dismounted his horse and turned to Talia.

"Your Majesty..."

SLAP!

Talia struck Captain Rollins across his cheek, cutting him off from speaking another word. Captain Rollins was stunned and did not turn his head back to Talia.

"Look at me!" Talia said with command.

Captain Rollins clenched his lips together.

"LOOK AT ME!" Talia shouted with force.

Captain Rollins turned his head to Talia. Talia's eyes were red and filled with tears. Captain Rollins could feel his heart break as he looked at the princess and her sorrow.

"You swore" Talia said taking a moment to compose herself "You swore after Tomlin was killed that you would never let another member of my family die. What happened? How did my father and most of your men get killed so easily?"

Captain Rollins mouth went slightly agape and a look of remorse came over him.

"We...." Captain Rollins said "They had taken the Banshee hostage."

Upon hearing this Talia was struck by confusion. "What do you mean they had the Banshee?" she asked.

Captain Rollins lowered his head slightly and his voice was shaken.

"King Alaois spoke to Lord McHarris peacefully for over ten minutes. We were on guard but he had a dark mage bring the Banshee out. She was tied and gaged, unable to speak or anything. We were all shocked by the sight as we never would have thought that they would challenge the harbinger of death. They took the gag from her mouth and the scream was so loud."

As Captain Rollins said that last word he fell to his knees and shook his head. Talia as well as the soldiers were shocked by the sight. Here was the fierce worrier Captain Rollins whom had survived countless battles on his knees in shame.

"I failed him." he said holding back the lump in his throat. "I failed him as I failed your brother."

Captain Rollins stared into the distance completely at a loss for words. Talia was unsure of what to do or say in this moment. She looked at Captain Rollins and though anger was deep in her heart over her father's death. She could only feel pity for the man before her. Talia slightly raised her hand to Captain Rollins stopping short and griping her hand into a fist. Talia let out and huff and placed her hand on the captain head. Captain Rollins looked up to Talia, surprised by her action.

"I forgive you." Talia said in a low voice of unease.

Talia took her hand away from the captain's head and turned away. She walked over to Samuel and asked to hold the baby in her arms. Samuel too was in a state of shock over Talia's quick forgiveness of Captain Rollins. As he handed Talia the baby Samuel said softy that she was quite quick to forgive him, though she had more right than anyone to be angry with him. Talia turned her gaze from the baby in her arms and looked to Samuel.

"It was quick for me to forgive him, and deep down I may never fully forgive him. But we need to prepare for war and he is the most experienced soldier in all of the kingdom."

It was at that moment that a small wooden bird flew down from the mountains. Talia and Samuel were taken back by this sight, but Captain Rollins recognized it. Standing to one knee Captain Rollins spoke.

"That is a song bird construct. Master Senan used them to help us spy during the last war."

The bird fled down to Samuel's shoulder and landed. The bird then opened its beak wide and Master Senan's voice echoed from it.

"Talia, Samuel, find Captain Rollins and make your way to my home. Hurry!"

Talia looked at Samuel "I think we should do as he said. Master Senan would not send a message like that unless it was important."

Samuel replied that maybe Master Senan had found the location of Emily. Talia nodded and asked one of the nearby soldiers to take the baby in her arms. The soldier ran up to Talia and took the child in arm.

"Take the baby back to my mother and tell her that this child was a rescued slave."

Talia then turned to looked at her father's body. She walked over to him and lifted the sheet from his face. Talia leaned over and kissed her father's forehead. Holding back a tear Talia asked that her father be taken back as well with a message.

"We are at war."

Talia placed the sheet back on her father's face and stood.

"Captain gather the men you came here with. Send them to all lords in the kingdom and spread word to raise their legions. Tell Lord Cillian That I want his men here at the pass. No one is to go through the gates."

Captain Rollins fully stood and turned to his men. Clearing his throat, he looked to the soldiers and shouted.

"You heard your princess! Send word to all lords to raise their legions."

Captain Rollins looked to Talia "Your Majesty, we must hurry to Master Senan's home. If he made a song bird construct the message, he has for us must be of great importance."

Talia, Samuel, and Captain Rollins mounted their horses and with great haste raced for Master Senan's home. Soldiers on horseback poured from the Black Mountain Pass Gate. They ran in all directions off to the many Lords of Dreegahnna. With the horses breathing heavily the thunderous roar of their hooves. What would normally take a full day's ride, but the trio made it within half that time. Talia, Samuel, and Captain Rollins tied their exhausted horses to the stone wall that sat at the base of the hill. As the trio made their way up the hill to the house, the wooden bird sat upon one of the window seals. As Captain Rollins Opened the door the wooden bird flew into the home and straight to the firepit in the center of the home. As the trio stepped into the home the bird flew into the dim flames that were upon a chard log. The moment the bird touched the flames, they grew in size. The fire roared near to the ceiling and began to swirl. As the flames shrank in size the image of Master Senan began to form in the flames. Talia, Samuel, and Captain Rollins gazed at the image as it formed, their focus broken only by Master Senan's voice.

"Talia, Captain..." the image said "I have given a part of my magic to this construct and once the bird full burns to ash my image shall fade. I have grave news, I found Aine but I fear her heart has been corrupted by the darkness of grief. She will not help us in her current state and we will need her help. My fear was realized as I spoke to her. King Balor has returned."

As the name left the lips of Master Senan's image Talia and Captain Rollins grew pale and wide eyed.

"Who is King Balor?" Samuel asked in confusion.

Captain Rollins turned to Samuel "How can you not know who the Dark King is?!" he asked Samuel with anger and confusion.

"ENOUGH!" shouted Talia "We do not have long to listen to the message, the bird burns more by the second. Samuel, I'll tell you later, please continue Master Senan."

Master Senan's image nodded and spoke.

"I don't know where he is but his darkness flows through her soul. He has promised her a gift that no magic can bring. The return of her son. You must find her crystal, the one that has her soul bound to it. Her soul was pure and clean of the darkness when she bound it to the crystal. When you find it, you must smash it and the light of her former soul will go to her body. The darkness will be purged from her heart and mind."

Captain Rollins looked at Talia "Your Majesty you have to return to the capitol. It is the only place we could defend easily from the Dark King."

Talia said nothing to Captain Rollins.

"Talia!" Captain Rollins said in a soft shout placing his hand on her shoulder.

"We have to find that crystal Captain." Talia said "We will need Lady Aine's power to even come close to defeating her. It took the combine might of Master Senan, Lady Aine, and my grandmother to defeat him. Us alone will not have that same chance."

Talia finished speaking as she turned to Captain Rollins.

"Samuel…" Master Senan's image said "I did find the location of your sister. She is indeed on the other side of the Black Mountains in a fortress. It is south of the pass surrounded by a small town. She is weak, for her blood has been used in a dark ritual."

Before Master Senan's image could say anymore and thunderous roar came across the land.

"MASTER SENAN!"

The three looked out the nearest window to the directions of the Black Mountains. Captain Rollins ran to the window and opened it looking to the mountains in the distance. He could see a beam of light come from the clouds above the mountains. Captain Rollins turned to Talia and said with fear.

"Talia, I beg you to return to the capitol now. Master Senan has fallen."

Talia's heart nearly stopped and she turned back to Master Senan's image in the fire.

"If I have fallen, then finding that crystal is your only hope." The image said "I know of its location in vague detail. It rests north in New Heavan, the Selkie guard it somewhere in the sea. I fear that my time is soon coming to an end for the song bird is soon to be ash."

As Master Senan finished, his image began to fade from the flames with a finale message.

"Goodbye Talia. You have become quite the young woman and will be a great queen."

As Talia watched the image of her longtime friend fade, a tear fell from her eye onto her blouse.

"I fear I have cried more tears on this day then I have in my life." she said wiping her eyes. "Captain take your men back to the pass and help Samuel find his sister Emily; I must go to New Heavan at once."

Captain Rollins had a look of shock upon his face.

"We cannot continue this rescue mission with all that has happened Talia!" Captain Rollins said excitedly "We need to plan for defense against the Dark King."

Talia stopped Captain Rollins.

"Our best defense will be to get that crystal from the Selkie. I can make the journey in a day if I ride through the night."

"A DAY?!" shouted Captain Rollins "Your horse would die of exhaustion before you even made it to the North. Not to mention the few roads going through the New Heavan Mountains are always heavy with snow fall."

Talia huffed

"We need that crystal if we are to have any hope of saving Lady Aine and fighting King Balor. I need you to help Samuel save his sister and see them home safely."

Captain Rollins grew enraged and turned to Samuel.

"Today's events rest solely on your sister being taken! You never did tell me how she was taken by the trolls! What was she doing? Did she go into the mountains? Did she deal in dark magic? Well?!"

Samuel did not know what to say and stood in silence.

"SPEAK! DAMN YOU!" Captain Rollins demanded

"Because she is human." Samuel said in a brief moment of fear.

Talia looked at Samuel in shock and he to her. Captain Rollins went silent with surprise, but it was to not last long. Rage filled Captain Rollins and he drew his sword. Samuel reached for his, but Captain Rollins was too fast for Samuel. The captain grabbed Samuel's hand and stopped it from grabbing the sword. The captain then took the hilt of his sword and punched Samuel in the face. Captain Rollins took Samuel's sword from its sheath and threw Samuel to the ground. As Samuel looked up, Captain Rollins stood with both blades crossed against Samuel's neck.

"Captain!" Talia shouted.

"No! I want to know everything this instant." Captain Rollins replied "Tell me everything and choose your words wisely."

Samuel looked over to Talia. She had a look of worry upon her and was unsure of what Captain Rollins will do. Samuel turned his gaze back to Captain Rollins and spoke

"Very well. Allow me to stand and I will tell you everything."

Captain Rollins paused then slowly backed the swords from Samuel's throat. With blade pointed to his neck Samuel stood slowly, keeping his gaze upon the captain.

"Now that you stand, look me in the eyes and speak." Captain Rollins said with blade pointed at Samuel's neck.

Samuel took a deep breath and nodded, Samuel held up his hand and showed Captain Rollins his ring. Samuel took the ring from his finger and the magic was undone. He stood before Captain Rollins and Talia in his mortal form. Captain Rollins glared at Samuel and asked.

"How does filth come in position of magic?"

Taking another deep breath Samuel explained everything to Captain Rollins. As soon as Samuel finished speaking Captain Rollins took pause. He then turned to Talia and asked

"How could you keep this information from your father and I?" Talia was unsure of how to respond to the captain question.

"I kept it from you and father out of a debt of gratitude to Samuel. He helped me fight the other humans that tried to take me."

Captain Rollins huffed.

"Be it as it may Talia. This human has cost this land its king and its most powerful mage. Now we have the Dark King to worry about as he may at this very moment be marching an army upon us."

"Master Senan told me before he left to find Lady Aine, that this was a trap." Talia responded harshly "That means they were planning on killing my father soon anyway. You yourself were surprised that they had the Banshee bound. This mission only had allowed it to happen sooner than later."

Captain Rollins gritted his teeth and threw Samuel's sword to the ground. He then sheathed his sword and rubbed the back of his neck.

"What reason could the Dark King have for a human girl? How old is your sister?" Captain Rollins asked Samuel.

"She is thirteen winters." Samuel replied.

"Has she reached womanhood yet?" asked the captain.

Samuel was stunned by the question. Captain Rollins explained.

"If she has and has had no relation with a man her blood is pure and could be used in certain dark magic. Now, has she?"

Samuel paused and thought of how he should respond. After a moment of silence Samuel nodded.

"Yes, she reached womanhood last month."

Captain Rollins let out a deep breath from his nose and turned from Samuel.

"Master Senan did say your sister had lost blood and was weak." Talia exclaimed "Captain what dark magic could use pure human blood?"

Captain Rollins shook his head.

"I'm not sure. But If King Balor used her blood, it can be for nothing good. That monster has for a long time been trying to take back his throne. It would have saved your father and I a great deal of sleep had your grandmother made sure he was dead."

Samuel and Talia could see Captain Rollins was deeply concerned about the information he had just been given. Samuel looked to Talia who stood with her arms crossed; a look of fear in her eyes. Samuel stepped over to her and placed his hand on her shoulder.

"Talia I cannot begin to thank you for all the help you have given me. I also cannot give a deep enough apology for all the heartache I have caused. Captain Rollins is right though, and you should return to your castle." Talia looked at Samuel with surprise as well as Captain Rollins. "Yes, you need to find that crystal but you also need to lead your people. Let your soldiers find the crystal and lead your people against this King Balor. I will find Emily on my own and we will make our way to the portal."

"And how do you intend to open the portal, Samuel?" asked Captain Rollins "Only those with magic in their blood may open the portal to the human realm."

Samuel thought and said that he would find a way. Captain Rollins lifted his head slightly and looked down at Samuel.

"Let me make sure Talia is safe behind the Captial walls and I will help you find your sister. I believe I know the fort and town Master Senan spoke of. But once we have her you will leave this land and never return to it again."

Talia looked at Captain Rollins and said that she can make it to Charwood and have Lord Cillian's men escort her home.

"You should go now to the fortress if the gate has not been laid siege to yet." said Talia.

Captain Rollins looked at Talia and gave a slight smile.

"Talia I am aware of your tricks you know? I will see you to Charwood and then I will help Samuel." Talia tried to speak but Captain Rollins would hear none of it.

"Come we must make haste if we are to make it to Charwood and back to the Black Mountains before nightfall." Captain Rollins said turning away and walking to the door.

"Talia" Samuel said in a soft voice. "I will be fine and so will all of this. You need to let your men find that crystal and allow the captain to do his duty."

"He has failed once this day and will have to live that for the rest of his life. Allow him to protect you and your kingdom."

As soon as Samuel finished speaking, he followed Captain Rollins out of the house and placed the ring back upon his finger. Talia stood looking at Samuel and Captain Rollins. She closed her eyes and clenched her hands into fists. Letting out a huff she followed the two outside.

"Captain, wait!" Talia shouted from the doorway of the house.

Captain Rollins and Samuel turned at looked at Talia emerging from the home.

"I'm sorry. I know I can be rash and sometimes I don't think things through. But I was young when Tomlin was killed and you have been there as a second brother for me."

Talia walked up to the captain and hugged him. Captain Rollins stood in shock and slowly embraced Talia back.

"I don't blame you for anything and you have done so much for not only this land but my family. I know your feelings against humans and I respect your opinions, but I ask you to please do this last thing for me not as you princess but as your friend."

Captain Rollins could feel the sincerity in Talia's words; He looked at her and then to Samuel.

"I want you to go back to the capital Talia. At least give me the sound thought that you are safe behind its walls." Captain Rollins said holding her tightly.

Talia let go of Captain Rollins and stood back.

"I will go back home." Talia said with heaviness in each word. "My father's body should almost be there and my mother will need me. Send the best men you have to New Haven and find that crystal. Make sure Samuel and his sister are safe back in the human realm before you return."

Captain Rollins took Talia by her shoulders and said that he will do this last request as a friend.

"Samuel mount your horse and ride to the pass." Captain Rollins said taking a badge from his shoulder armor. "Show this to the men there and tell them I will be there shortly once Princess Talia is safe. You WILL wait for me there."

Samuel nodded and looked to Talia.

"Talia" he said with a small shiver in his voice "This may be the last time we see each other. I want you to know that you are the only person I consider a true friend."

Talia was taken back by Samuel's words and stood silently. Samuel walked over to his horse and mounted it.

"Captain, please make sure she is safe."

Captain Rollins said that is his priority. With one final goodbye Samuel rode off to the Black Mountain Pass. Samuel's mind raced as he thought of all that he had seen and done so far. His journey soon to come to an end in this land and he a bit wiser from it. But the thought remained of how this land was to soon be torn by war and its beauty to be destroyed. Beauty, that word stayed in his mind and the image of Talia appeared. Something about her made Samuel feel alive. He had had more adventure in his life than he ever had because of her. He will never forget her nor the sacrifice that her father gave so that he may find Emily. As Samuel drew near to the pass, he could hear the sound of men shouting.

"Could the attack from the trolls be happening?" he thought.

As Samuel drew closer it became clearer that the gate was indeed being attacked. If he could get through to the other side of the mountains however, he would still be able to find Emily. Samuel could see smoke rising from above the trees. One of the four towers of the gatehouse was a flame, men were firing arrows from the small section of wall. Lord Cillian stood shouting at some men who were running with buckets of water to put out the flames. He saw Samuel approaching and shouted

"Samuel! Where is Princess Talia and Captain Rollins?"

Samuel dismounted his horse before it even stopped running. Nearly tripping he caught himself and looked at Lord Cillian.

"Captain Rollins is taking Talia back to Charwood so that your men can escort them back to the Captial." Samuel said while still breathing heavy from the ride.

"Good. Her safety is paramount right now. The people need the bloodline of Arina Dreegahnna to survive if they are to have any hope. My friend did you find your sister?" Lord Cillian replied.

"No, His majesty the king was killed before we could find her. But Master Senan gave me a location; Captain Rollins gave one of his badges and told me to show it to the guards here and wait for him. Speaking of the guards what happened here? Is the gate under attack?" Samuel asked.

Lord Cillian huffed

"I wish. I would love to get revenge for them killing my dearest of friends. No this is only the beginning; A rider came with flaming spear and threw it though one of the arrow slots on the tower. The wooden floor inside the tower was dry and caught fire immediately. I've ordered the gates sealed with stones, but that damn fire has gotten so big we cannot get near the gates."

Samuel looked at the blaze and asked if there was a way he could help. Lord Cillian replied

"Yes, grab a bucket and help the men fight the fire."

Samuel nodded and rushed over to the soldiers in the bucket line. They pointed to a well and gave him a rope and wooden bucket. Lord Cillian took a rag from his pocket and wiped his brow as watched the flames. Captain Rollins then rode to Lord Cillian on horseback and leaped down.

"Are we under attack?!" he asked in fear.

Lord Cillian told him the same thing that he had told Samuel. Captain Rollins shook his head

"Reinforce this gate and let no one through, other legions will be here soon."

Lord Cillian nodded in acknowledgement and said that he has two ballistae coming from Charwood's armory.

"Good" replied Captain Rollins "I'll see to it that some catapults are brought here as well. You should tell your people to make their way to the capitol where it is safer. We can reinforce the walls there with both ballistae and catapult. If laid siege to the capitol can hold for months, it has its own water wells and some of the residents grow small gardens."

Lord nodded and shouted for one of his soldiers to come to him. One of the soldiers handed off his bucket of water and ran over to Lord Cillian. The soldier saluted by placing his fist over his heart and shouted.

"SIR!"

Captain Rollins looked at the soldier and told him to go to Charwood and evacuate the town to the capitol. The soldier saluted once again and ran to a nearby horse that was hitched to a post. With a loud shout the soldier rode hard in the direction of Charwood. Captain Rollins turned his gaze from the soldier ridding away to Samuel. Samuel was hurriedly pulling bucket after bucket of water from the nearby well.

"Samuel!" shouted the captain.

Samuel looked over to the captain and handed over the rope to another soldier. Samuel walked over to the captain and Lord Cillian.

"Captain, if you'll excuse me, I must help finish putting out the fire and fortify the gates." Lord Cillian said walking away.

As Samuel reached Captain Rollins, he asked how they are to get through.

Captain Rollins looked at Samuel and then to the pass.

"Once the fire is out, we will move quickly through the gates. I fear that they may have an army on the other side of the mountains already. If so, I am sorry but your sister will no longer be a priority."

Samuel was taken back by the captain's words.

"I'm sorry but my first priority is to the safety of the people here in this land. I know I gave my word to Talia but her safety is higher than that of your sister."

Though Samuel was angry at this statement he understood that the safety of everyone would indeed take presidents over Emily. He had seen how many of the fairy folk are treated in the Black Mountains and did not wish for that to happen to the kind people of Dreegahnna.

"Captain" Samuel said with firmness "How do I get to the fortress Master Senan spoke of?"

Captain Rollins raised his brow

"Do you intend to rescue her alone? You will be killed if they catch you."

Samuel said that the captain was needed here in Dreegahnna more. One person could move more quickly and quietly then two. Captain Rollins thought of Samuel's words a huffed through his nose.

"Go through the pass and turn right, the town you seek is a day's walk from there. The fortress sits at the base of the mountain and is small. It was used as a supply station during the war. But if they have your sister there then there may be more guards now. There is an old sewer gate behind the fortress, it is small but a man could move through it. That is your way in and out."

Samuel thanked Captain Rollins and began to turn away to the gate. Captain Rollins grabbed Samuel's arm, stopping him.

"I swear if anything you do over there brings more harm to this kingdom anymore then it has. I will make it my duty to make you pay for it."

With that Captain Rollins let go of Samuel's arm. Samuel turned back to the gates which now were no longer on fire.

"Open the gates and let him through!" Shouted Captain Rollins.

As Samuel walked to the gates Lord Cillian stopped Samuel and wished him luck and to stay safe. Samuel thanked Lord Cillian and walked through the large wooden gates which promptly closed behind him.

CHAPTER SEVEN

Now alone on the other side of the gates Samuel could once again feel the chill of the mountains bare down upon him. It felt otherworldly as he passed the spot where Talia had held the body of her father the king. Samuel stepped lightly as he feared another attack on the gates. The Black Mountain Pass was narrow and had nowhere to hide if someone came. Each step he took echoed on the jagged rock face walls that stood highly on both sides of him. The crunch of the dirt path beneath his feet made his heart beat greatly. Soon the smell of the salt air from the ocean reached his nose and he could hear the sounds of it washing over its beaches. As Samuel emerged from the pass his heart seemed as it was going to beat out of his chest.

"Now I go right." He thought to himself.

Samuel looked at the dirt road branching to the right. It seemed to snake along the base of the Black Mountains leading South. Samuel began to walk with his thoughts on getting Emily as far away from this land. He walked at a brisk pace for the day was half passed done and he wanted to try to reach the town before nightfall. Samuel walked for hours, passing abandon homes that were falling apart. Some showed signs of the previous war, scorch marks, rusty axes and swords lay everywhere.

"It must have been a small yet ferocious battle." Samuel said out loud to himself.

It was then that heard the sound of hooves beating heavily behind him. Samuel looked around and hurriedly ran into the ruins of a stone barn. As Samuel hid amongst the moss covered stone a rider flew by on horseback. The rider wore a black cloak that flew in the wind and the cling of his spurs rang out. As the rider rode away, Samuel stood and stepped out into the road with his gaze fixed on the ridder. Samuel looked down and saw that the rider's horse had left hove prints in the dirt.

"He's ridding hard to somewhere." Samuel thought.

Samuel continued to follow the dirt road keep an eye for the hove prints of the ridders horse, and an ear for anymore ridders. As the sun began to set Samuel could see a large square tower looming over a small town at the base of one of the mountains. This was the town and the small fortress that Samuel had been searching for. A small stream flowed from the mountain side next to the fortress.

"That must be the drain the captain was speaking of." Thought Samuel.

The sun was setting and its orange haze made the tower glow over the rooftops of the town. Its long shadow seemed to creep up the mountain.

Samuel left the straight path of the road leading into the town. Knowing he would be spotted quickly he made his way into the forest that surrounded the town. Making his way through the forest, he kept the town in sight. Samuel could see the ridders horse from earlier, tied to a post outside of a small inn. Samuel made his way to the side of the building and looked around the corner. The rider stood speaking to a troll dressed in plane clothing, next to him was a short man in a red frock coat and black boots.

"Alaois is dead." the rider said to the others; Samuel listened closely. "We have orders to form garrison and move on the pass. The Far Darrig are to support the supply lines leading to the pass; The rest of us will be forming in Vera. King Balor is going to force a portal into the old Capitol and we are going to take it back."

"Force a portal?!" asked the leprechaun in the red frock coat. "Is that possible?"

The ridder laughed and said that it was and that was how they had taken the human girl for the ritual. *Emily?* thought Samuel. What disturbed Samuel the most is he still did not know what ritual would use her blood. Either way Samuel could not delay any longer and silently moved to the back of the building from the direction he came.

Samuel could see the stream coming down from the mountain. He used it as a guide as he made his way through the narrow back streets of the small village. Torches began to light the town as Samuel moved swiftly. In a way he was thankful for the extra light lending him vision in the dark, but he was afraid as well. He now had to be more cautious as the light could expose him. Dark mages, trolls, leprechauns, and fairy slave soldiers walked by. Samuel hid the best he could behind barrels, crates, and corners of buildings. His boots seemed to clack upon the cobblestone streets with each step, making his heart race. With a few close calls; Samuel had finally made it to the edge of the village. The tower fortress sat high above all and the stream seemed to be turned into a mote in front of the fortress. To the side of the fortress Samuel could see and iron gate four foot in height and three foot wide. He now had his entrance, but was unsure of how he could get to it. The gate sat on the other side of the stream and a twenty-foot gap between the building Samuel was hiding behind. Soldiers stood guard at the front gate of the fortress; well within view of where he needed to go.

The only saving grace Samuel had at this point was the area he was in was dark. However, he still had to cross a flowing stream which could many feet deep. He had to take the chance though in order to make it to the gate. Staying low to the ground while still on his feet. Samuel moved swiftly in the dark and made his way to the edge of the stream, his eyes never leaving the soldiers standing guard. Once at the edge of the stream Samuel sat down upon the edge and lowered his feet into the water. The water near came to his knees, but it was shallow enough to walk across. Still staying low and looking all around, Samuel moved slowly through the waters. Each time his leg made a sloshing sound, his heart near stopping each time this happened. Samuel nearly slipped on the slate rock in the stream and grabbed the opposite embankment for support. Samuel turned his head to see one of the soldiers looking slightly in his direction. Samuel's eyes widened as the soldier turned towards Samuel and began to squint his eyes, trying to find the source of the splashing noise. The soldier took only a few steps before shrugging the noise off to be an animal.

Samuel let out a sigh of relief and rolled onto his stomach. Grabbing the edge of the embankment his pulled himself up from the stream. His boots stood full of water, but he could not stop to empty them here. He hurriedly made his way to the gate and lifted it up. Its hinges made a squalling sound from years of rust. As the noise began to grow Samuel laid on the ground and crawled under the gate. The moment Samuel was under the gate he slowly let it back down. The smell of the sewage below him took him immediately. Trying to hold back the urge, Samuel leaned against the wall of the drain and removed his boot to drain the water. After he had done so, Samuel began walking in a crouch down the darkened corridor of the drain. Samuel could hear the distant sound of people speaking to one another. The torch light from a small hole at the base of a wall; shined down into the sewer where Samuel was. Samuel peaked through the hole and saw three trolls sitting at a table drinking ale and eating some potted meat. They were laughing and making merry, the smell of the potted meat floated down to Samuel. It was a pleasant reprieve from the foul stench below him.

He had to press on into the darkness until he found a room not occupied by anyone. Samuel did have a sword, but would be no match for a trained fighting force. Samuel held his hands high on both sides of the sewer walls to feel for an opening in the walls. He soon found another opening with no light in the room, Samuel crawled through the hole into the dark room. A door sat to Samuel's right as he crawled into the room. The light came through every crack and notch of door. Samuel quietly and cautiously opened the door enough to peek out; light illuminating his eye as he did. A long stone brick hallway lay on the other side of the door. A single torch burning on a wall mount. Samuel opened the door more and leaned his head into the hallway. Looking one direction which ended at a wall, he was the left with only one option. Careful to make no noise, Samuel stepped into the hallway and drew his sword. Samuel's heart pounded as he walked down the long hallway. He came to a split in the hallway and leaned out to look down both corners.

Samuel's heart stopped as he leaned around the corner a servant girl with chains around her wrists connected to her neck stood before him. She fell back to the ground and began to breath heavily as if she was about to scream. Samuel dropped his sword and grabbed the girl; placing his hand over her mouth.

"Please don't scream." Samuel said in a hushed voice. "I am looking for the human girl and if you help me find her. I swear that I will take you to the other side of the mountains to Dreegahnna where you can be free."

The girl's eyes widened as Samuel said this. "I'm going to lower my hand and let you go."

Samuel's hand lowered and the girl's breathing had slowed. No sooner had Samuel's hand fell from the girl's mouth and she slapped him across the face.

As Samuel was stunned by the girl's action, she screamed allowed. "Help! Intruder!"

The sound of boots and armor came from behind Samuel down the hallway. Samuel ran in the opposite direction away from the girl and boots. As Samuel rounded a corner a soldier stood there with sword and shield. The soldier was stunned by the sight of Samuel, Samuel took advantage of this situation and charged the soldier with his shoulder. The soldier was knocked back to the ground as Samuel tackled him. Samuel quickly stood and the soldier grabbed his foot. Samuel fell to the ground and looked back to the soldier. Taking his other foot, Samuel kicked the soldier in the face, breaking his nose. As the soldier reared in pain Samuel hurriedly made it back to his feet and ran. He found himself at a dead-end hallway with a few rooms to his sides.

Thinking quickly Samuel ran into one of the rooms; a broom sat to his left inside the room. Samuel grabbed it and wedged it into the bottom of the door to act as a stop. Samuel looked around and found that he was in the kitchen of the fortress. It sat empty for the moment, but a pot of stew boiled above the fire and he knew someone would be there soon. Samuel had to find Emily quickly as the servant now knew of his intentions.

"Why did she scream?" Samuel thought *"I told her I would help her to freedom in exchange for her help."*

Samuel did not have long to think however as the sound of footsteps came from the other side of the door. Samuel reached for his sword only to find an empty sheath. He had forgotten in the cayuse that he had dropped his sword. Samuel looked around and grabbed a large cleaver that hang on the wall. The door was forced open to reveal a large troll clad in armor, he stood so tall that he had to duck just to enter the room. Samuel was astonished at the size of the troll, giving the troll time to knock the cleaver from his hand. The moment the blade struck the ground the troll punched Samuel in the face. The force from the punch was so great that Samuel was knocked immediately to the ground. His vision was dazed and blurred, blood pooled from his lips and nose. As Samuel laid on the stone floor the troll grabbed him by his trousers and lifted him as though he were a sack. The troll stepped out of the kitchen with Samuel in hand and threw him at the feet of several soldiers.

"Take this fairy filth to the dungeon." The troll said in a rough deep voice.

The soldiers grabbed Samuel by each arm and dragged him away.

Samuel could barely keep his eyes open as the blow from the troll was so powerful. The soldiers did not take long in taking Samuel to the dungeon of the fortress. One of the soldiers opened an iron door and reviled a dark room with a single narrow window high upon the wall out of reach without a ladder. The light of the moon was the only thing giving some light to the dark room. The soldiers took Samuel and chained him to the wall next to the door, his arms held above his head. Once the shackles had been fastened, the soldiers left the room shutting and locking the iron door they had come through. Samuel tried looking around but found it difficult to see straight or even a few feet in front of him. It was as if the darkness of the room enveloped him and nothing could be seen that was not in the moonlight of the window.

"They beat you up pretty good, didn't they?" A small voice said from the darkness.

Samuel looked for the source but could see nothing. The sound of a chain dragging across the stone floor came from the other side of the room. Samuel tried to focus in the direction of the sound but his vision just could not focus.

"A troll in armor struck me in the face. It's hard for me to see at the moment, I beg your pardon." Samuel said in response.

The sound of chains moving once again filled the room.

"You need not beg any pardon sir. I've heard the soldiers call that troll general and have heard he has won many a fight. He and other men in dark hoods held me the other day and cut my hands. That troll held me upside down until I passed out. When I awoke, I was in this room chained to the wall. My hands had cloth wrapped around them and I was told I will be kept here if they need more of my blood."

Samuel slightly raised his head and his vison seemed to be stabilizing to a small degree.

"Take your blood?" Samuel asked.

The voice said that the men in dark hoods spoke of a spell.

"I fear these men are in league with devils and are practicing dark magic." the voice said. "You sir, what are you? And elf?"

Samuel smiled slightly and let out a small laugh.

"No" said Samuel "I am human. The ring upon my finger hides who I am from the creatures outside this room."

Samuel then reached over to his finger and pulled the ring off. The shackles upon his wrists cutting into the base of his hands as he did so.

"I don't know how well you can see in this darkness, but I have removed my ring. I am now human in appearance as I was, they day I was born."

The sound of the chains moving across the room seemed to move slightly closer.

"Samuel? Is that you?" the voice asked with surprise.

Samuel thought and raised his head.

"Heaven forgive me for not recognizing her. Emily?" Samuel asked excited.

"It is! Samuel how did you get here?! How did you get that ring?!" the voice of Emily said with joy.

Samuel slipped the ring back onto his finger and told Emily that he would explain his journey when they are safe. For now, they had to find a way to break free of their chains.

"I have tried Samuel, there is no way to break free of them." Emily exclaimed with sadness. Samuel sat against the wall and slouched.

"What can we do to get out of here?" He thought to himself.

Samuel could not see much in the darkened room; he could barely see Emily on the other side of the room. It was then Samuel remembered the coin he had stowed in his pocket. If he could somehow reach it, he could use it to turn the screw of the shackle locks and free himself. But his hands were bound above his head against the wall. He could never reach his pocket

"Emily" said Samuel still trying to find a way to get the coin. "I have a coin in my pocket. If I could reach it somehow, I could undo the shackles upon my wrist. But My hands are chained above my head. It may take me some time."

Emily's voice then came from the dark. "Try to hurry brother."

Samuel shrugged and said he would try, but he was chained in such a way that he did not think his hand could reach. Samuel stood and the best he could and still could not reach into his pocket. His fingers barely came to his waist with the shackles holding them. Samuel then braced his foot upon the wall and contorting body so much, just reach his pocket that the shackles began to cut his wrists. With the tips of his fingers Samuel could touch the top edge of the coin. With a mighty grunt Samuel managed to grab the coin with his two fingers.

Trying not to allow the coin to slip as blood was trickling down his fingers. Samuel carefully pulled the coin from his pocket and grabbed it in his blood-soaked hands.

"Did you manage to grab it?" Emily asked.

Samuel was in pain as the air stung the cuts of his wrists.

"Yes" he replied taking a moment to relax his arms from bending so much. "I cut my wrists doing so, but the coin in in my hand. Give me a moment and I will try to turn the shackle screw."

Samuel bent over trying to turn the screws of his shackles. The blood from his wrists made the coin slip many times and Samuel feared that he may drop the coin. After several minutes of turning slowly, the screw lock of his shackle on his right hand fell to the ground with a heavy clank.

"What was that?" Emily asked.

Samuel told her that his right hand was free and he would hurry and try to free his left. Samuel began to turn the screw on his left shackle when footsteps could be heard coming towards the iron door of the dungeon.

"Samuel hurry! They are coming!" Emily said excitedly in a hushed voice.

Samuel began turning the screw like a mad man, with each turn the sound of footsteps drew closer to the door. Soon the light of a torch could be seen flickering in the crack below the door. Samuel only had a few turns left before the left shackle was undone. The sound of the wooden brace from the other side of the door being removed sent fear into Samuel and Emily. Right as the door opened Samuel managed to undo his shackle. As a soldier stepped in Samule hid behind the door which opened inward. As the soldier stepped in Samuel grabbed him from behind. The soldier fought by elbowing Samuel in his ribs, but Samuel did not let go. Though his hands covered in blood, his grip around the soldier's neck was fierce. The soldier then tried to use his torch and burn Samuel away. He swung it wildly at Samuel and near hit him a few times. The soldier gasped for air as Samuel squeezed his throat. Soon the soldier began to slow in his movement and the torch he had been carrying fell to the stone floor below.

It was then the sound of a large pop echoed in the room. Samuel fell back onto the ground and sat down. Still holding the soldier and breathing heavily he let the soldier go. The light of the torch illuminated the right side of his body, giving him an, other worldly silhouette. As Samuel sat upon the ground catching his breath he looked over to the direction of Emily.

"I'm sorry you had to see that. I am also sorry that I didn't go with you that day to the market. Had I not been so concerned with stoning the field we would have never been here."

Emily stood and replied to Samuel's statement.

"Even if you had gone with me, how would you have stopped me from being taken? Perhaps it was meant for you not to go with me and you to save me."

Samuel nodded and stood. He searched the guard and found the turn key for Emily's shackles.

"We need to hurry." Samuel said picking up the torch and walking over to Emily. "They will notice when he does not return."

As Samuel undone Emily's shackles, she asked how they were to escape. Samuel looked up at Emily and said that he had slipped into the castle via a drain system and that if they could make it to a room where it was, then they could make their way out. Samuel grabbed the sword that was on the hip of the dead guard and held it tight.

"Emily stay close to me. I don't want us to get separated, we must find our way out."

Emily took Samuel's words to heart and grabbed his shirt to stay close to him. Samuel, with his new blade pointing the way. The two made their way down the hallway leaving the torch behind so as not to give themselves away to any other guards. Each step Samuel and Emily took seemed to echo on the stone walls of the fortress. The two came to the end of the hallway and not wanting to repeat what had happened before. Samuel used the reflection of the sword to see around the corner of the hallway. Several doors lined both sides of the hallway, a single torch again gave light to the darkened halls. No light came from any of doors that lined the hallway and gave Samuel a relief.

"Stay close. We have a few rooms to look into in this hallway. Be careful when looking and don't make any noise. Look on the bottom edges of each wall for a small arched opening. That is the drain system we can escape through." Said Samuel looking back at Emily.

Emily nodded in acknowledgment and let go of Samuel's shirt. Samuel turned back to the hallway and rounded the corner, stepping slowly and keeping his blade at the ready. He and Emily began to slowly open each door, the clank of each door latch unlocking made their hearts freeze. Fearing that the sound of which would give them away to a nearby enemy. One by one each room was searched and each held no drain. Emily soon found a water closet and saw a drain at the base of its wall.

"Samuel, I think I found the drain you spoke of. It is in this water closet and wrecks of excrement." Emily said.

Samuel closed the door to the room he had been looking in and stepped over to Emily. He looked inside the water closet and saw the drain that Emily had spoken of.

"That's it." Samuel said stepping inside the room.

Emily paused and asked if that truly is the drain, they must use. Samuel said that it was and that she should not think of it or its smell.

"If you do think of the smell imagine it is from the animals on our farm."

Emily gave a slight cringe at the thought, but pressed on as she wished to return home and leave this place. Samuel lowered Emily into the drain and then followed after her. The smell became more powerful in the darkness of the drain and Emily gagged a bit. Samuel held his arm over his nose and mouth.

"It does smell, but we must press on. This drain will take us out of the fortress into a small stream. From there we will make our way back to the pass of the mountains and hopefully we can get through."

As the two began to walk in the darkness Emily asked Samuel how he found her.

"Emily, I want to answer you, but we must stay silent for a moment." Samuel said swiftly.

The two soon could hear the running water of the stream and hope began to fill their hearts. The gate of the drain came into the view, the shimmer of the water reflected on the bars as the moon gave illumination to them. Samuel lifted the gate up and told Emily to go through and stay close to the fortress walls so as not to be spotted by any guards. Emily nodded in acknowledgment and kneeled under the gate. As soon as Emily was outside, Samuel followed behind her, carful to lower the gate slowly so as not to make noise. Samuel, staying low turned and looked around.

"I do not wish for us to try and sneak through the town. That was how I got into the fortress." said Samuel in a hushed voice "We shall have to cross the stream and make our way to the forest. The stream comes to my knees, so it will be almost to your waist. I want you to ride on my back and hold tight as we cross. If we go at the same time, we have a greater chance of not being spotted."

"Samuel" Emily replied "The moment we make it to the forest you must tell me everything. I fear for your soul that you are using magic."

Samuel was unsure of how to respond to Emily, giving only a nod of acknowledgement Emily then hoped onto Samuel's back.

"Hold tight." Said Samuel as he slid down into the stream.

With each slosh of the water below his knees Samuel and Emily's hearts raced. As they made their way across the stream a guard from the fortress walked across the top of the towering structure.

"Samuel! A guard." Emily said in a hushed worried voice.

Samuel told Emily that they had to press on and could not stop as time was running out.

No sooner had Samuel reassured Emily, and an arrow planted itself into the ground. Samuel and Emily looked back and saw the guard on the roof of the fortress with his bow drawn and grabbing another arrow.

Thinking fast Samuel grabbed Emily and threw her to the other bank of the stream.

"Run to the forest!" Samuel shouted.

Emily, almost stumbling ran to the darkened forest. Samuel made his way through the water as more arrows rained around him. He looked over his shoulder to see more guards had joined in firing arrows at him. As Samuel reached the embankment and arrow pierced his right leg. Samuel shouted in pain as the arrow head sunk deep into his leg.

"Samuel!" shouted Emily from the safety of the forest.

Samuel lifted himself out of the stream and began to run as fast as he could with the arrow in his leg. Arrows continued to fall around him, one even missing his head by mere inches. As he reached the forest, he leaned upon a tree gritting his teeth from the pain. Emily ran to her brother and looked over his shoulder to the fortress.

"Samuel look!" she said with worry in her voice.

As Samuel turned several guards emerged from the stream bed and began to transform. Snouts grew from their faces and fur began to cover them all over.

"Demons!" said Emily with fear.

Samuel shouted run and they began to run as fast as they could into the forest. As Samuel and Emily ran into the darkness, the pain of the arrow in his leg made each step agony. It was then that a spine-chilling howl rose across the air and the sound of many feet beating upon the ground gave rise to fear in Emily and Samuel. Samuel looked around and a large tree stood silhouetted against the darkness; only given illumination by the moonlight.

"Emily" said Samuel trying to catch his breath "Up this tree. Stay silent once you are there and don't move."

Samuel helped Emily up the tree by boosting her up. He followed suit and began to climb but it was too late. Right as he began to climb one of the wolves ran up to him grabbed his leg. Samuel looked down to see that the wolf had transformed back into a guard.

"You're not going anywhere filth!" The guard shouted.

Samuel tried to kick the guard away, but this only enraged the guard. Seeing the arrow in Samuel's leg he grabbed it and twisted it. Samuel let out a harsh scream and fell from the tree. Emily shouted for her brother as fell in pain.

The guard looked up at Emily with a smile.

"I see filth sticks together, a fairy and a human. Perfect for each other."

Right as the guard finished a blade burst from his stomach. The guard looked down to find Samuel had drawn his sword and stabbed him. As the guard fell Samuel made his way to his feet.

"Samuel, behind you!" Emily shouted.

Two other guards grabbed Samuel and slammed him to the ground. A third guard came and began to climb the tree for Emily. Emily broke a small branch and began swinging it wildly at the guard. Right as the guard grabbed Emily by her leg and arrow pierced his throat. Emily's eyes grew as the guard gagged on his blood and fell from the tree. The two other guards looked at the fallen guard's body and up to Emily. It was then another arrow struck one of the guards in the chest and fell back from holding Samuel. Samuel managed to shove the last guard from his back and punched him in the face. The guard shrugged it off and hit Samuel back and the two became fully embroiled in a fist fight.

"Samuel, drop!" Shouted a male voice from the darkness.

As Samuel did so an arrow burst from the darkness and planted itself into the eye of the last guard. As the man fell to the ground dead Samuel looked into the darkness to see the shape of a man coming towards him.

"I thought you may need my help." the figure said. Samuel recognized the voice as that of Captain Rollins and breathed a sigh of relief.

"I feared that my sister and I was to die at this moment." Samuel said leaning against the tree his sister was in. "Emily, it is safe now. He is a friend."

Emily slowly climbed as Samuel slid to the ground. He had lost much blood from his wound and had fought hard with the pain. As Emily landed with a final jump to the ground, she could make out Captain Rollins.

Fear filled her "Samuel he is one of them."

Samuel shook his head and reassured Emily that he was a friend and nothing like the others. Emily still had fear in her heart and was wary of Captain Rollins. Captain Rollins could see the arrow in Samuel's leg.

"We need to pull the arrow out and wash the wound with boiled water. We cannot do that here so I suggest we make haste back to the pass."

Captain Rollins said as he helped Samuel to his feet. Samuel looked at the captain.

"I overheard some mean speaking of an attack. They intend to use something called the Far Darrig to hold their supply lines."

Captain Rollins gave nothing but a small hum in acknowledgment and said that they are like leprechauns but eviler in their ways.

"They would sell their own mother for a coin and tell her she was going holiday just to have a laugh."

Captain Rollins said as the three began walking in the dark. Samuel held tight around Captain Rollins neck and huffed with each breath. Captain Rollins asked if they had said anything else. It was then Samuel had remembered the attack on not just the pass but the capitol.

"I heard them say that when they attack the pass, King Balor will open a portal and attack the capitol."

Captain Rollins froze with Samuel's words. He then turned his head sharply to Samuel.

"When is the attack to happen?!" he asked with haste.

Samuel shook his head and said he was not sure.

"It could be happening now. We need to save Talia and her mother the Queen."

Captain Rollins then looked to Emily and under his breath uttered. "Is that the reason for her blood?"

Captain Rollins mind was a flood with thoughts as he tried to make sense of the situation. He then said that he had brought his horse and another for them to make it back to the pass quickly. The horses were tied to two small trees at the far edge of the forest opposite direction of the fortress and town. Captain Rollins helped Samuel to his horse's mount and then helped Emily onto the same horse.

"You will have to help guide his horse." Captain Rollins said hand the reign to Emily. "Your brother has lost much blood and has become weak. Follow close behind and do not slow for anything, we will get him help once we are safe on the other side of the mountains."

Emily had had enough and demanded that her and her brother be sent home.

"It was your kind that held us in that dungeon. Why should I trust you?" she said holding Samuel.

Samuel tried to calm Emily, but she was to have none of it. Captain Rollins had not yet mounted his horse and stood looking up at this small girl demanding answers. He walked over to his horse and mounted saying nothing. As soon as he fully sat down upon his horse, Captain Rollins looked to Emily.

"You should trust me because your brother saved a girl that is dear to me." Emily paused and hung on Captain Rollins words.

"I can never pay him back completely for that, but I can make sure that his leg is treated and you for whom which he ventured all this way to save are safe. Now follow me."

With that Captain Rollins began to ride and Emily sat briefly in silence.

"Emily" Samuel said faintly as tried not to pass out "Follow him."

Emily was filled with fear, but the fear of her brother being lost was greater and with reluctance she followed close behind Captain Rollins. The trio rode at a quick pace but not so fast that Samuel would be bounced too much and lose more blood. It did not take long before they had reached the gates of the Black Mountain Pass. But as Captain Rollins, Samuel, and Emily would soon find out. Hatred for human kind in Dreegahnna was alive and well.

CHAPTER EIGHT

The gates of the pass creaked open as the trio passed through. Lord Cillian sat on a log covered in sweat as Captain Rollins, Samuel, and Emily came through the pass.

"I am beyond glad that you are all well." he said wiping his brow "The fire was put out shortly after you went after Samuel. Speaking of whom I see he has found his sibling."

Lord Cillian stood and walked over to Samuel and Emily. As Lord Cillian drew closer, he could see the blood dripping from Samuel's leg and the arrow protruding from it.

"Good heavens Samuel" Lord Cillian said in surprise "Get some hot water and bandages!"

But as soon as Lord Cillian stood next to Samuel's horse and began to help him down, he saw Emilly better in the torch light.

"You..." he said slowly "You're human! Captain Rollins what is the meaning of this?!"

Captain Rollins dismounted his horse and said that they had gave their word to help him save his sister.

"Yes, but that was before we knew that his sister is human!" Lord Cillian shouted.

He then demanded to know what witch craft Samuel was using to hide his true form. Samuel though weak tried to speak in his defense.

"It is the ring.... given to me by..." Samuel could hardly finish his sentence as he had become weak and limp.

Lord Cillian scoffed at Samuel and turned his attention to Emily. "You girl, do you have any idea what you have caused this land?!" Emily flinched back as Lord Cillian scolded her.

"Because of the expedition our king undertook to help save you, he is now dead as well as several good men."

Captain Rollins then intervened on Samuel and Emily's behalf by stating that this murder of the king was long planned and they had nothing to do with it. Lord Cillian turned to Captain Rollins and told him to mind his place. Captain Rollins was shocked by this as he had known Lord Cillian for many years, and had never been at odds with him.

"You failed in your duty to protect the king when he was in Vera. Now you return with a human and a liar whom uses magic to deceive us?!"

Captain Rollins looked up to the soldiers standing on the wall, their eyes focused on Lord Cillian and his words. Some sneered, others did nothing and stood silent.

"Captain Rollins have you not heard the stories of what their kind has done to ours?! How they hunted us for greed of gold or of magic?!"

Captain Rollins then told Lord Cillian of the attack coming on the pass.

"I'm aware of the attack coming, hence why I am here with my legion! But that does not solve the problem of that sits before us."

Captain Rollins then said ten words that shook Lord Cillian to his core. "King Balor intends to open a portal to the capitol."

Lord Cillian stopped and went pale where he stood. He looked at Captain Rollins and then to Emily with his mouth slightly agape.

"When?" was the only word Lord Cillian could muster.

Captain Rollins said that he was unsure of when it was to happen, but would most likely be soon. Lord Cillian huffed through his nose a licked his teeth slightly.

"Captain I will go to the capitol with some of my men. The leprechauns will be here soon with Lord Fionn and they will hold this gate with the remainder of your men and mine. Put both of them in irons and be ready to move out." Lord Cillian said with authority.

Captain Rollins looked to Samuel whom was slumped over his horse passed out from the blood loss. Emily sat afraid behind him holding onto her brother.

"I will not put them in irons." Captain Rollins said.

Lord Cillian paused and looked to Captain Rollins.

"You are a soldier in his Majesties Legion. I am a LORD, A GENERAL!! Compared to you. You will do as ordered."

"I!" said Captain Rollins loudly "I am Captain of his Majesties Elite Royal Guard. I take my orders from the Royal Family. Yes, you have sway over the legions and can even command my men in my absence, but Princess Talia gave me direct orders to see that Samuel and his sister are safe. I will see them to the portal quickly and make my way to the Capitol."

Lord Cillian was clearly angry at this statement and turned to look at the men manning the wall.

"How many of you are willing to help a human?!" Lord Cillian shouted "Remember they would capture, enslave, and use our ancestors for magic and gold. They are no better than the trolls and dark mages and far darrig whom right now on the other side of those mountains have our people in chains."

The soldiers stood silent and looked to one another. Some looked down and some stared intactly at Samuel and Emily. Lord Cillian then turned back to Captain Rollins.

"You, see? Even they know it is wrong to help a human. Does the Princess even know what creatures we have been helping?"

Captain Rollins replied that Talia does indeed know about Samuel and Emily being human. Lord Cillian was shocked by this news.

"The Princess was able to see past her hate and was willing to help someone in need. Not to mention he saved her from bandits when they first met."

Lord Cillian huffed at Captain Rollins words.

"One good deed does not make amends for a history of violence against our people! It saddens me that the princess was taken in by a simple good act, and yes it was a great act to save her. BUT! It makes no difference! This only proves that Talia is still a child and needs more time to develop before she could ever sit on the throne."

Captain Rollins became enraged by this statement and slapped Lord Cillian across his face. Lord Cillian held his jaw and looked at the captain in shock.

"Need I remined you of your place Lord Cillian?!" Captain Rollins shouted "Need I also remind you that Queen Arina Dreegahnna was three winters younger than Princess Talia when she fought King Balor and founded this land?! Now I will be taking Samuel and his sister Emily to the portal without your help and return to the Capitol to get the Royal Family out before the attack."

Captain Rollins turned and grabbed the reign of his horse and tied a rope from it to Samuel and Emily's horse. Captain Rollins mounted his horse and looked back to Lord Cillian.

"Take your men and go to the Capitol. You will hold it and the castle and pray I do not repeat what you have said to the Queen Mother Roisin."

Lord Cillian remained silent as Captain Rollins spoke. The captain then turned his horse and began walking at a quick pace away from Lord Cillian. As they made their way down the road Emily spoke.

"I still have doubts, but thank you for what you said and did back there. I think I speak on behalf of my brother as well."

Captain Rollins looked over his shoulder slightly and replied.

"I still have some doubts myself. A lifetime of prejudice does not go away easily and sometimes it never goes away. But your brother did save Talia and has showed no ill intent towards her or us. His only focus has been finding you and taking you home."

Emily responded "Still, for what it is worth. I thank you, but what of Samuel? He has passed out from his wounds and we still have not treated it."

Captain Rollins stopped his horse and dismounted. "Get off the horse and make me a small fire. Be quick about it."

Emily dismounted her horse but was confused as to why Captain Rollins needed a fire.

"I am going to treat his wound how many of us treated them during the last war. We don't have clean water to treat the wound so I need a fire to do so."

As Captain Rollins said this, he took Samuel from the horse and laid him on the ground. Emily hurriedly grabbed some small sticks from the side of the road and made a small fire by striking two stones together. Captain Rollins ripped Samuel's trouser leg open around the arrow.

"Good, the blood has begun to clot. That will help with what I'm about to do. Hand me a thick stick."

Emily handed Captain Rollins a stick and placed it into Samuel's mouth. He then drew a small knife from his belt and placed the blade in the fire.

"This will hurt your brother briefly, but it will buy him time as you two make your way back to your realm. You need to clean the wound with boiled water when you return home or he may lose his leg to infection."

Emily nodded as she listened to the captain. Captain Rollins grabbed the shaft of the arrow and pulled hard, removing it from Samuel's leg. As he did Samuel grunted in pain and bit down on the stick in his mouth. Captain Rollins then grabbed his knife from the fire and pressed the blade to the wound. Samuel bit down harder on the stick nearly biting it in two. Emily sat in shock at the site of her brother's pain. Captain Rollins took the blade from Samuel leg and returned it to his belt. The armor on his body gave protection from its heat. He then stood and kicked dirt on the fire, putting it out.

"Now, let us get you two home."

Captain Rollins grabbed Samuel and placed him back onto the horse. Emily then mounted the horse with her brother drabbed over before like a blanket. Captain Rollins mounted his horse and began leading them.

"Thankfully we are close to the portal. I'm sure it all seemed strange to you when you first came through here." Emily had a confused look and said that she had never been through this land before. Captain Rollins looked back to her and asked

"Surely you must have? I'm sure in all the confusion you didn't realize it."

Emily replied that she had been brought through a portal in the very fortress she had been held.

Captain Rollins was confused by Emily's words.

"*Then what would they have needed your blood for?*" he asked himself.

This thought was the only one that repeated itself in his head. Soon they reached the hill that the portal was at and climbed to the top where the large rock was. Captain Rollins stopped the horses and dismounted.

"Samuel said he had been given help by two dwarfs named Magdalen and Alister in your world. They must not be far from the portal and you should seek their help in treating your brother. I will open the portal and see you off, but I must make haste to the Capitol."

As he said this, he helped Samuel down from the horse followed by Emily. As Emily held her brother over her small shoulder, she looked at Captain Rollins and asked if he would be punished for striking Lord Cillian. Captain Rollins slightly smiled as he walked over to the large stone.

"No. I suspect that he will try to find a way to take revenge for it, but he would never tell the Queen or Talia. He spoke ill of Princess Talia, though it was in rage. Take my advice be careful of what you say or do even when angry. Now let us send you home."

Captain Rollins drew the symbol of the Celtic Knot upon the stone and the portal opened with a gust of wind and a swirl of light. Emily was taken back by the different lights and colors that swirled before her. The last time she had been taking through a portal she had been in a large sack.

"Hurry through and find help for your brother." Captain Rollins said as he mounted his horse.

Emily looked back to the captain with her brother draped over her shoulder, then to the portal. She slowly stepped through dragging her brethren's feet behind her. The different colors seemed to embrace her as she walked through; she was both amazed and a little scared of the sight. Emily looked behind her to see the portal close and the sight of Captain Rollins disappear. Emilly pressed on dragging her brother's unconscious body, the portal opened before her and she could see a forest with a large clearing. As Emily stepped through the feeling of nausea set in and she had to let Samuel fall from her shoulders. Emily fell to her knees and began dry heaving as she had had very little to eat in days.

As Emily began to regain her composure she looked around. The forest seemed to loom over her and the rising sun gave light to a thin fog rising from the clearing she was in. Emily lifted herself up from the forest floor and grabbed her brother. She only made it to the edge of the clearing, but after carrying her brother through the portal and dry heaving she could not carry him anymore. Emily looked around but could think of a way to carry her brother.

Biting her lip, she looked into the forest and then back to her brother. "I will return for you Samuel. I have to find help."

Emily lifted Samuel's head and shoulders and leaned him against a tree. She then took the ring from Samuel's figure returning him to human form. Emily took Samuel's sword and began walking into the woods. The morning sun shined beams of light through the tree tops. The sounds of birds chirping filled the air as Emily walked, giving her some semblance of calm. She walked for a couple hours in the forest unsure of many sounds that seemed to surround her. Her thoughts were of Samuel though and how he had braved everything to save her. It was the that the smell of smoke filled her nose. This gave Emily hope as it may be the very dwarfs that Captain Rollins had spoken of. Emily followed the smell and soon saw a small campfire surrounded by men. Emily found comfort that they were all human and began walking towards them asking for help.

"Please help. My brother is hurt and lies wounded in a meadow nearby." she said drawing closer.

The men looked at her taking their eyes from some small morsels of food that they had in their hands. "

Please he needs help!" Emily shouted once again.

The men looked at each other, with one motioning for the others to follow him. The men stood and the man who motioned began walking with a limp.

"Show us where he is girl."

Emily grew happy as them men stood to help, she told them to follow her and led them to the small meadow where the stone was. As the group made their way into the meadow the men saw Samuel's unconscious body laying against the tree. As they walked over to him, Emily said that he had been shot in the leg with an arrow and that she had used fire to close the wound.

"That's smart of you las." The man with the limp said as he kneeled down to Samuel.

He began to dig through Samuel's pockets and found the gold coin in his pocket.

"Only one?" the man said with disappointment.

"What are you doing?" asked Emily "Why are you searching my brother? Please help him."

The man stood while looking at the coin.

"I think maybe the girl may have more on her, or at least some value."

Emily's heart began to race as she realized these men were not here to help, but rob her and Samuel. Emily began to back away slowly as the men began to slowly surround her.

"How about it last? Got anymore coin on you?" another man said as he walked behind Emily.

It was then that one of the men shouted out in pain. The other men looked to see a small older woman with red hair holding a large branch. She had struck one of the men knocking him out.

"If ya want to go after any girl here then come after me!" The men laughed.

"George has a habit of getting knocked out, doesn't he?" The man with the limp stated "Put the stick down dwarf. Maybe we won't kill you slowly for hitting our friend."

As the man drew closer the woman swung the branch, only for it to be grabbed mid swing by the limping man.

"That was a bad move." The man said with a slight smile.

The woman smiled back and stamped on the man's foot. The man let go of the branch and shouted, grabbing his foot. The moment the branch was free from his hand the woman clubbed him on his head.

The man fell to the ground grabbing his head shouting "Kill her!".

Two other men in the group drew small knives and began moving towards the woman. That was when Emily grabbed a branch as well and struck one of the men from behind. As he fell the other man looked back in surprise and began raising his knife to stab Emily. The small woman threw her branch and struck the man in his back, knocking him to the ground. The woman ran over to Emily and said to grab her brother and follow her. Emily nodded and grabbed Samuel dragging him. The woman jumped in and began helping Emily drag Samuel away from the meadow. The group of men staggered to their feet and began looking around for Emily and the small woman.

"Spread out and find that hag!" The man with the limp shouted.

Emily and the woman huffed as they dragged Samuel through the forest. "My home is not far from here. We need only press on a bit more." the woman said panting heavily.

"This is the second time I've carried this young man. He shall need to carry me soon."

Emily looked at the woman and was surprised by the statement. Soon the outline of a small cottage began to appear through the trees.

"There! Quickly now child." said the woman.

The two made their way into the cottage and laid Samuel on the floor. Both of them huffing from carrying him through the forest. The woman shut the door to the cottage and latched a large bolt at its center.

"Now dear" she said finally catching her breath. "Let me get a look at your brother. Where is he hurt?"

Emily explained that he had been shot in the leg with an arrow and someone had helped him by burning the wound. The woman looked over Samuel's leg and the shuffled over to a pot of water hanging next to the fire.

"This water is not boiling, but it is hot enough to clean the wound."

The woman then grabbed a small rag from a nearby drawer and began dipping the rag into the water. She began wiping the wound and said calmly to Emily.

"I take it you're Emily?" Emily's eyes grew at the woman's question and she nodded her head slowly. "A few months ago, he came through here. He had been knocked unconscious by a falling branch in a storm. My late husband Allister helped me drag him here and we gave him food and directions to the meadow where I found you. My name is Magdalen dear forgive my manners."

Emily became confused by Magdalen's statement.

"How can it have been a few months ago? My brother and I were only gone for a few days."

Magdalen smiled and told Emily that in the other realm a day is equal to a month in the human realm. Emily was shocked by this revelation as she had felt very little time had pass. Magdalen finished treating Samuel's wound and with Emily's help laid him in the small bed he had been before.

"Come dear. Let's leave your brother to rest and have us a nice cup of tea." Magdalen said while putting her arm around Emily.

Many hours passed before Samuel began to stir. He sat up on the bed with a grunt as the strain on his wounded leg moving hurt greatly.

Samuel quickly recognized the room that he was in and took great comfort in knowing that he had made it back. Emily entered the room and smile quickly came over her face. She ran over to Samuel and hugged him tightly around his neck.

"Thank God you're okay." she said holding back the urge to cry.

Samuel smiled and embraced Emily.

"I had quite the journey in order to find you. I'm glad you are safe, but how did we make it back here?"

Emily explained all that had happened from the time he had passed out. Samuel was amazed that Emily was able to carry him upon her shoulders. The moment Emily finished her explanation, Magdalen walked into the room. A smile filled her wrinkly face as she looked at Samuel and Emily. Samuel looked to Magdalen and smiled, and with a small grunt stood from the bed. He limped over to her and hugged her as one would an old friend.

"It is good to see you again. I cannot begin to thank you for the help you gave me. Why didn't you tell me that you and Allister where..." but Samuel could not finish his question as Magdalen placed her hand on his chest.

"Shhhhhh. I didn't tell you for I wanted you to know that looks can be deceiving and that help can come from those who have kindness in their hearts. You were frightened when I walked into the room for you thought I was a creature of magic."

Samuel looked to the ground and smiled "I was indeed a fool about many things when I first met you."

It was then Samuel remembered all that had happened. He grabbed Magdalen by her shoulders and asked if she could open the portal to Dreegahnna. Magdalen was surprised by this and asked what the matter was.

"Talia is in grave danger. I have to help her."

Magdalen was shocked by Samuel's words and asked how Samuel could know Princess Talia Dreegahnna. Samuel summarized his journey for Magdalen and pressed the matter again that he must return to help her. As Samuel said this, he tried to walk past Magdalen but fell, catching himself on the door. Magdalen and Emily grabbed Samuel and told him he has lost to much blood and needs to rest.

"Talia Dreegahnna will be fine. She has an army of loyal soldiers willing to fight for her. You need rest." Said Magdalen pushing Samuel back to bed.

"Samuel please listen to her. You're too weak to make any journey or fight."

Samuel slumped back down on the bed and let out a large huff. Emily reassured Samuel that all will be well in the morning. Magdalen grabbed Emily's arm and began leading her back out of the room.

"Come child. Let us give your brother some rest and I suggest you get some as well."

Emily and Magdalen left the room and allowed Samuel to rest. Samuel lied, staring at the ceiling thinking only of Talia's safety.

"God in heaven" he said in a low breath "I know my faith has waned in the past few years. I know I have not attended your house as regularly as I should. But I ask you to please keep her safe."

Samuel was right in the things he said. He was not as devoted as Emily was, but he still held out hope that someone would hear and answer his prayer. A few days passed and Samuel began to regain his strength. He was saddened to learn that Magdalen's husband Allister had passed. Every morning Emily, Samuel, and Magdalen sat down and had breakfast together before doing the days chores.

"I think we should be heading home soon." Emily said taking a bite of her eggs.

Samuel nodded and joked that he had to sell their chickens and the goat in order to buy a rusty sword.

"I bought that sword to save you and lost it when I made it to the castile."

Emily smiled and said that Samuel would be foolish enough to lose it. Samuel leaned on the table and breathed a sigh through his nose.

"I am happy you're finally safe Emily. I will see you back home and mend the farm, but I feel I must return to Dreegahnna."

Emily dropped her spoon and looked at Samuel.

"It is not our place Samuel. As Magdalen said Talia will be fine."

Samuel gritted his teeth at his sister's words. It was then Magdalen grabbed Samuel's hand.

"Samuel, I served Lady Aine under the reign of Arina Dreegahnna. I knew King Alaois when he was a prince. From the stories I've heard of her, he raised her right and she has the same fire her grandmother had. Trust in when I say she will be fine and they will beat The Dark King once again."

It was at that moment a knock came at the door. The three looked to the front door and Emily.

"It may be the bandits we ran into."

Samuel stood and grabbed the iron poker from the fire.

"If so, I will defend as you two run."

Samuel slowly approached the door as Magdalen and Emily backed into a corner of the room. Samuel grabbed the door handle as another knock came and he looked back to Emily and Magdalen and nodded. With a swift action Samuel opened the door, iron raised only to find Talia. Samuel's mouth went agape and he dropped the iron from his hand. Talia stood with her clothing ripped and her face was half covered in blood. The second Talia realized Samuel stood before him tears began to flow from her and she grabbed Samuel with deep embrace. Samuel hugged her tightly and helped bring her inside. As soon as Magdalen saw Talia, she became excited and began hurriedly cleaning the room.

"I apologize your majesty for the mess. I will have it clean in a jiffy." Talia held up her hand and told Magdalen to not do so. "Please, just a chair and some water." she said wiping her eyes.

Samuel pulled up a chair as Magdalen poured water into a small copper cup.

Talia took the cup and drank it quickly as she sat down in the chair.

"I told Captain Rollins the plan I heard. Were you able to fight off the attack?"

Talia was visibly shacking as she held the cup in her hands.

"May I please have some more water?" she asked holding her cup out.

Magdalen replied of course and poured Talia another cup. Emily sat down and took a small rag that lay on a table next to her. She wetted the rag and handed it to Talia. Talia looked to Emily and smiled

"Your brother did a lot to save you."

Talia took the rag and began wiping the blood from her cheek. Samuel placed his hand on Talia's shoulder and asked again had they managed to fight. Talia took another drink from her cup and looked at Samuel. Her eyes became misty but she did not cry.

"I don't even know where to begin." she said wiping her right eye.

Samuel took his other hand and grabbed Talia's hand.

"Start where you left my side."

Talia nodded and began to tell her story. A story though not long, would send a chill through the soul of any and all who heard it.

CHAPTER NINE

"I went with Captain Rollins back to Charwood." Talia began "As we rode, he kept telling me to not pursue Lady Aine's crystal."

Talia rolled her eyes at Captain Rollins statement.

"I'm serious Talia. Your mother will need you now more than ever and we cannot afford for anything to happen to you. I cannot afford for anything to happen to you."

Talia let out a ha and smiled. Captain Rollins looked over his shoulder to Talia on her horse.

"What is funny about what I said?"

Talia looked through her brow "Are you worried about me or your reputation?" she said shaking her head.

Captain Rollins turned back to the front of his horse and sighed.

"I never meant for your father to be killed on my watch. He was like a father to me as well considering mine was killed in the dying days of the rebellion."

Talia rolled her eyes again and shook her head.

"You showed your devotion well." Talia scoffed.

Captain Rollins stopped his horse and turned it to face Talia. He had a serious look upon his face as he looked at her.

"I grew up with Tomlin." Captain Rollins said with slight force.

Talia asked him to stop speaking but Captain Rollins replied with a firm no.

Talia became surprised and looked wide eyed at the captain.

"I grew up with him and he was a friend and a brother. Against your father and mothers wishes he wanted to be a soldier and follow in his family footsteps. I joined with him and we traveled all over this land. When the Trolls tried to retake this land, we fought in many battles. Your brother brought decisive victory at the battle Hagon Port in the south. We moved north in order to prevent them from running and refortifying themselves. We walked right into a village where they were waiting."

Talia once again asked Captain Rollins to stop but he continued.

"For two days we fought. For two days we did not sleep or eat, all we did was take each house, each street. I took a spear to my hip and an axe strike to my back. When I fell your brother quickly slayed the two goblins that that had struck me. A troll came from nowhere and tried to strike him from behind. He was quicker though and took the troll's head. That was when a dark mage appeared and despite me crying to him, I watched him die in a blast of fire."

Talia bit her lip and began to shake. She gripped the reign of her horse so tight that the leather could be heard.

"Hours later I looked your father in the eyes when he arrived with reinforcement, holding your brother's body! I had to tell him I had failed to protect my friend, my brother, his son! He shook his head and told me I had not failed, that I had fought bravely and because of your brother and I we had stopped one of the largest advancements into the kingdom. I watched as your father, with tears falling from his face picked your brothers body up and he carried him away. After that day I swore I would do whatever it takes to payback the debt I owed to your family. Your father founded the Royal Elite Guard a few weeks later after the peace had been signed and of all the veterans in the kingdom, he chose me to lead it. I took the position as a way to pay him back to pay Tomlin back. I failed in that duty at your father's side I admit. I should have seen the trap the moment we walked into Vera. You can hate me for the rest of your life, but I will be damned if I let you, the last direct descendant of Arina Dreegahnna die while I am still Captain. This is the one and only time I will ever speak to you in this manner Talia. You will go home to safety and be ready to lead your people in the coming war by your mother's side." Captain Rollins finished and turned his horse around and began ridding again.

Talia was angry with Captain Rollins but could bring herself to say nothing further. She followed close behind him as they made their way to Charwood. As they arrived in the town, soldiers hurried around and civilians were loading carts with furniture and cloths. Captain Rollins shouted to one of the soldiers to come to him. The soldier ran to him and looked up at him, then to Talia. Upon seeing Talia, the soldier bowed his head and turned back to the captain.

"Has Lord Cillian been informed of the situation?" Captain Rollins asked.

The soldier replied yes and that he ordered the town to evacuate to the Capitol until it is safe.

"Many veterans of the last war volunteered to take up arms again sir. They are going to escort the people to the capitol."

Captain Rollins told the soldier to see to Talia and make sure she made it home safely.

"Where is my father's body?" asked Talia.

The soldier swallowed and looked to Talia, he than raised his arm and pointed to a cart surrounded by soldiers and men whom had taken pitchforks as weapons. Talia dismounted her horse and began walking to the cart. Captain Rollins told the soldier to finish his duty in Charwood and gather men to fortify the pass. The soldier saluted Captain Rollins and ran off to see to the people. Captain Rollins looked over to Talia who was now at the cart where fathers body was. She had her hand placed upon his chest and the older soldiers around her were holding back tears. Captain Rollins was resolved in that moment. He would never again allow for another member of the Dreegahnna family to fall by his neglect. Captain Rollins then rode away from the town of Charwood to catch up with Samuel and ensure his promise to Talia. Talia watched as Captain Rollins rode away, her feelings distorted by lose and anger. Though the captain had failed her and she was indeed angry with him. Talia knew that at heart he always had the best interest of her family. She looked to her father's lifeless body and said in a low whisper.

"Papa I'm sorry I always disobeyed you. Rest easy as mother and I will lead this kingdom."

One of the older men standing guard saluted Talia with a thump of his chest.

"Your Majesty" He said in a stoic voice. "I served in your father's legion during the last war. I may be older than what I was, but I can still fight and ask your permission to stand as your guard to the capitol."

Talia turned to the man and looked at him. He was a man around the same age as her father. A man in his mid-fifties with salt and pepper hair, a large scar ran the length of his face. He stood well over six foot in height and was very broad in build. Talia looked to the other older men that stood around her and her father's body. They ranged in height, age, gender, and species; Leprechauns, Fairies, and Pooka stood all around.

"Did you all serve in the last war?" Talia asked.

Everyone standing there nodded and replied yes, an old Pooka soldier with small horse ears and grey hair braided into a pony tail said that no matter how old any of them were, if they can hold a blade, they would fight for the kingdom that freed their families. Talia smiled slightly and lowered her head.

"Then I grant you all the title The Old Guard. As long as you are willing to fight you may serve." Talia said with a smile and tear.

Everyone standing there saluted and the old soldier that had asked Talia's permission to fight said that they should see her and her father home. Talia swallowed as she nodded her head. Talia looked over to a younger soldier and told them to send a group of four men to New Heaven in the north. Many of the soldiers old and young were confused by this order and one asked why a small group of men should go there. Talia looked to the soldier who asked the question

"Before he died, Master Senan told me that Lady Aine was alive and we had to find her crystal in New Heavan in order for to have her full power."

The older soldiers were shocked by this news and looked to one another. Four older soldiers immediately volunteered for the mission and said they would not return without the crystal in hand. Talia nodded and told them to go as quickly as they could. The older soldiers saluted and ran off to find horses and gear for their journey. Talia knew that Aine had been corrupted by King Balor and she had to keep this fact a secret. If the people of Dreegahnna had found out that one of the very people who had freed them had turned, they may lose hope.

"*Hope*".

That word stuck in Talia's mind, she hoped her land would be safe, she hoped Samuel would find Emily, and she hoped that this war would be short. Four old Pooka transformed into horses and had themselves hooked to the cart that King Alaois's body lay. In total the old soldiers numbered around twenty and all stood guard proudly. Husbands, wives, and children hugged and kissed their family members whom now took up arms. Talia looked at the old soldiers and asked who had the highest rank during the last war. The soldiers mumbled amongst themselves and an old Leprechaun stepped forward.

"I was a Lieutenant in the last war your Majesty. My name is Oisin."

The leprechaun stood around three foot in height and had brown curled hair. He had large mutton chops on each side of his face. He wore chainmail upon his body and a helmet similar to the ones other soldiers wore. The only difference in it was a brass band that surrounded the brim and a large dent in the right side. Talia nodded and told the soldier that he would take charge of the Old Guard and led them back to the Capitol. The leprechaun saluted and asked to drive the cart that had her father. Talia agreed and the two mounted the cart.

"To the Capitol with haste!" Oisin shouted with a snap of the reign.

The group began to leave Charwood as many of the younger soldiers began to fortify the town and prepare for the worst. The civilian's whom had been packing hurriedly to leave all stopped and bowed their heads as Talia and her father passed. Many of whom were visibly shaken by the death of their king. The Old Guard followed close behind the cart falling into rank and column. It was then that civilians with carts and large sacks upon their backs began to follow behind. Some younger soldiers walked beside the large group of people, but most stayed behind to fight any coming threat. The sun had fully set by mid-way through their journey to the Capitol, but they dare not stope for fear of attack. It was around midnight when the group reached the Capitol. The large wooden gates to the city opened and Talia breathed a sigh of relief as the cart entered.

As the cart moved through the main street of the city many people flocked to see if the rumors of their king's death were true. A woman dropped a basket of laundry she was carrying into her house as she saw the king's body upon the cart. A man whom stood near by the statue of Arina was shocked as his mouth went agape. Soon both sides of the street were filled with people, all of whom were crying as the body of their king went by. Talia fought with all her strength not to cry anymore, but the emotions of her people struck hard and a tear fell from her eye. Oisin saw the tear fall from his Princess's eye and grabbed her hand. Talia looked at Oisin and he to her. Oisin leaned slightly to her and said.

"Your Majesty I know I cannot say nor do a thing to change that which has happened, but take comfort in knowing that you are not alone in your grief. For the people of this land love your family so."

With those words Talia could not hold back any more and began to cry completely. Upon seeing her distraught many of the people standing to the side of the rode fell to their knees. Some held one another, others turned away wiping their eyes. The cart as well as the Old Guard soon arrived at the castle gates. A soldier looked down from the gate house and was shocked by what he saw. Holding back his emotions he shouted for the gates to be opened. As the cart pulled into the castle grounds the main door to the castle flew open and Queen Roisin burst through. The moment she saw the king's body she shouted with a devastating wale. Talia jumped from the cart as it came to a stop and she ran to her mother. Talia hugged her mother tightly and the Queen returned the hug with tears in her eyes.

"Mama I'm sorry I let this happen." Talia said, now crying heavily.

Queen Roisin hugged Talia tightly and looked to her husband's body. Swallowing her tears, she told Talia that it was not her fault in any way.

"I was told all that had happened on your journey. I know you had no way of knowing what would happen. Where is Captain Rollins and your friend Samuel?"

Talia wiped her eyes and said that Captain Rollins and Samuel had stayed behind to find Samuel's sister.

"Master Senan, before he died. Told us where to find her." The queen nodded as she listened to Talia and then hugged her again.

"Oh, my dear child, the baby you sent ahead is here. I swear you are the kindest being in all the realm."

Queen Roisin then looked to the older soldiers standing guard over her husband's body.

"I recognize some of you. You served my husband in the last war."

The older soldiers saluted Queen Roisin and said they will always serve the liberators of the realm. Queen Roisin smiled while tears still fell from her eyes.

"Please take my husband's body inside. We will have him lay in state before the throne."

The older soldiers nodded to the order and carefully lifted the king's body from the cart. The queen turned to another soldier and said to grab the best table in the castle for her husband to lay upon. This soldier too nodded and saluted the queens request and hurried off to find the best table he could. When the young soldier ran away Talia looked to her mother and said that they must prepare for any coming attack. Queen Roisin nodded and grabbed Talia by her head.

"I'll see to the outer walls; I want you to stay here and direct refugees that I send here."

Talia shook her head and told her mother no, that she should see to the outer walls. Queen Roisin was having none of it though, she shook her head repeating no.

"Talia, I have lost your father this day I will not lose you as well."

Talia begged her mother to listen to her but she was interrupted. A soldier who stood on the walls of the castle shouted.

"Your Majesties! The town squares!"

Talia and Queen Roisin ran to the gates and looked to the town square. It was as if the air itself was shimmering, like the waves of heat on a hot summer's day. Queen Roisin became terrified and shouted for the gates to be closed and for all soldiers to prepare for battle. She then grabbed Talia and looked her directly in the eyes.

"Talia, I want you to hide in the castle. It is not safe out here." Talia tried to interrupt by her mother didn't let her "I know you are an accomplished sword fighter and could easily fell a dozen men, but that is dark magic outside these walls. You and I are no match for that. We have to hold this castle until help arrives."

Queen Roisin looked to a soldier closing the gates.

"You! Find anyone who is a light mage and able to fight. I want this castle sealed now!"

The soldier saluted and ran into the castle to find a light mage. Queen Roisin looked at Talia again and said for her to go, she then let go of Talia and ran to the gatehouse of the castle walls. Talia watched as her mother ran into the gatehouse and bit her lip while clenching her fist.

"Damn it!" Talia shouted as she turned to go into the castle.

Lightning sparked from the sky as dark clouds rolled over the capitol. It was then dozens of troll soldiers, goblins, dark mages, and fairy slave soldiers poured from the portal that had opened in the town square. Soldiers of the Capitol and the Elite Guard rallied and formed shield walls on each street. Their swords and spears meeting the dark army head on. A dark mage leaped into the air as fire flew from his hands, setting a group of soldiers on fire causing them to break rank. The dark forces began destroying buildings and fighting erupted between every house, on every corner. The fighting was merciless as the people of Dreegahnna did not want the dark army to take their homes.

The dark army was resolved to win this battle though and fought with absolute blood lust in their eyes and hearts. It was then a large arrow struck a goblin in the chest pinning him to a wall. Soldier nearby looked and saw a ballista on top of the castle walls being loaded to fire again. Queen Roisin stood by its side and shouted for all archers and ballista to fire upon all enemy soldiers. Though a force like rain fell from the sky of arrows and bolts, the dark army did not stop fighting. The numbers of the soldiers of Dreegahnna began to wane and Queen Roisin shouted for all remaining soldiers to make their way to the castle. A soldier nearby nodded and blew a brass horn that he had upon his side. Talia ran to a window and watched down from a tower. She could see many dead and fighting soldiers and civilians in each street. It was then the cry of a baby shook her from the sight. She looked over to the bed in the room and saw the baby that she had sent home laying upon it. Talia stepped away from the window and picked the child up and began to comfort it.

"Child, I hope you know only peace in your life time."

Talia walked back over to the window holding the baby and watched as fires erupted all over the city. The last of the soldiers of Dreegahnna ran into the castle walls and barricaded the doors. They stacked carts, rocks, tables, chairs, barrels, and the dead against the door in order to block it. The archer rained arrows upon the dark army relentlessly.

"Your Majesty!" shouted one of the soldiers.

Queen Roisin looked at him as he told her they were running low on arrows and she should take shelter as the fighting will soon be on the walls. Queen Roisin shook her and said that she will not let the kingdom fall under her watch and will stay and help fight. She threw off her robe and stood only in her nightgown, tearing the bottom off to allow for movement of her legs she asked for a sword and shield.

"LOOK!" shouted another soldier.

Everyone whom was not fighting turned to look in the direction the soldier pointed. The town square was a blaze but a lone figure could be seen in the fire and smoke.

"Someone has come to our aid!" shouted a soldier.

A large magical presence could be felt in the air. Queen Roisin leaned on the wall, trying to make out details of the figure. It was then a bolt of fear ran through her body and she could feel nothing but darkness coming from the figure. One of the soldiers looked to the queen and could see the fear in her eyes as she looked on. The soldier then turned his head and looked at the figure. The figure stood ten feet in height, but was not thin. Nay, the figure was broad in build as though they were of normal size. The figure then began to walk down the bloody and burning street leading to the castle. A wounded soldier of Dreegahnna whom had not made it off the streets saw the figure and held out his hand for help. The figure stopped and slowly looked to the bleeding soldier and held their hand over him. It was then a bolt of intense lightning shot from the figures hand and struck the soldier, causing his head to explode.

Queen Roisin and the soldier jumped at the sight and the soldier shouted for the ballista to fire on the figure. The men on the ballista turned the large cross bow to the figures direction and fired. The figure held up their hand and the arrow stopped in midflight. It then turned around and was shot back at the ballista with such force; The ballista exploded and those around were killed in the blast. As the figure drew closer to the castle, soldiers of the dark army bowed and made way for the figure. Talia stood in the window of the tower and watched in fear.

"That power" she whispered to herself "It could only be the Dark King." The moment Talia said this a voice came from over her shoulder. "It is, and he will reign supreme over all as he did before."

Talia turned with the knife from her waist drawn only to find no one. Talia was confused and looked for the source of the voice. It was then a sharp pain permeated through her neck, causing her to drop her knife. Talia shouted as she realized the baby was biting her, and blood began to fall from her neck.

She pulled hard and dislodged the baby's mouth from her neck to find that the baby had transformed into a small, grey imp with pointed ears and yellow eyes. The creature smiled as its mouth was covered in Talia's blood.

"You stupid Faries are weak." The imp shouted "You couldn't hold your city against the might of King Balor and you were too stupid to see a changeling when one was handed to you."

Talia's eyes grew wide as the imp tried to claw at her. It was as if a wild animal was in Talia's hands. She threw the imp across the room and it landed on all four on the ground and hissed at her. Talia looked to her knife that she had dropped and so did the imp. The imp smiled and darted for the blade, but Talia was quicker and grabbed it. She thrust the blade into the eye of the imp and in let out a horrific wale as the blade drove in. At that time members of the Old Guard burst into the room, led by Oisin. He had a small sword in hand and looked as Talia still had the blade drove into the imp's eye.

"Your Majesty!" he shouted.

Talia looked to Oisin and said that they had to get her out of the castle quickly. Talia stood and asked what had happened. Oisin shook his head and in that moment Talia's heart stopped. She ran to the window and looked down to see the gatehouse of the castle gone. Dead soldiers lay everywhere, some burning and some eviscerated. It was then she saw her mother being held by her neck by the figure from before. The Dark King Balor! Now that he was closer, Talia could make him out in greater detail. A crown of tarnished gold sat upon his head and was fused with his skin.

A large red eye sat in its center above his brow, matching his bloodshot eyes. Making it seem as though he had three eyes in total. A stained white long sleeve shirt with holes sat under a rusted chainmail tunic. A worn and torn cape of red and black hung from his shoulders held by two iron clasps. His boots where worn and black as coal and his trousers brown with patchwork. His skin a pale almost grey color with old healed wounds upon his face. Most noticeable was a large scar that ran the length of his left jaw. Many civilians whom had fled to the castle watched in horror and were begging Balor not to hurt Queen Roisin. Balor looked at the groveling people and then back to Queen Roisin. The queen was gasping and looked him in the eyes.

"We defeated you before."

Balor said nothing and the red eye on his crown began to glow. Queen Roisin began to scream as an intense heat began to come from inside her. It was then flames burst from her eyes and mouth and then her whole body exploded.

Raining blood upon the terrified people watching. Everyone screamed at the sight, but the scream that seamed the loudest was Talia. As she screamed one of the old soldiers grabbed her and put their hand over her mouth.

"Princess please!" He cried as he pulled from the window. "If that monster were to know we are here he would kill you without hesitation."

Oisin looked at the other soldiers and told them to find a safe route out of the castle.

"We need to get her to safety." He said as they ran from the room.

Talia cried and moaned heavily as the large soldier holding her kept hold of her mouth. Each corridor of the castle was in panic, soldiers barricaded doors, people were on their knees praying. It all seemed unreal to Talia as she was pulled to safety, her life in the castle was over and she was now a fugitive. Oisin and the old soldiers took her through a door leading into a small court yard behind the castle. A towered stronghold stood in the center of the wall.

"There! We can escape through the archery windows on the other side." Oisin said as he hurried to the door, however the door was locked and they had no time to find a key.

One of the old Pooka soldiers told Oisin to stand back and she turned into a large horse and kicked the door in. The group hurried inside and barred the door closed.

"Find some rope and we will lower each other out the windows." Oisin said grabbing a torch and lighting it.

The building was old and full of dust and webs. A soldier grabbed a rope from a barrel nearby and they hurried to the second floor. Talia was still distrait and had to held as they guided her up the stairs.

"There, there Princess. It will all be well in the end. You'll see. The Lords will come with their legions and we will beat the Dark King. Your family shall be avenged." The soldier guiding her said as they climbed the stairs.

Oisin and the soldier with the rope threw open the wooden shutters of the window and lowered the rope down. A soldier grabbed hold and leaped from the window, repelling from the second floor to the ground. The soldier looked up to the window and shouted that it was clear and they could send the princess down. Oisin looked to Talia and motioned for her to come to the window. Talia shook her head and with tears in her eyes she muttered she could not leave.

"Your Majesty you must." Oisin said with worried tone.

It was at that moment that a large thud came from the door down below them.

"They're here!' The large soldier next to Talia said.

"All of you protect the stairs. Your Majesty you're coming with me now!" Oisin cried as he grabbed her hand.

Using a bit of magic Oisin held Talia tightly and they leapt from the window. The rope seemed to come alive and wrapped itself around them, setting them down onto the ground gently. Oisin huffed as he landed and with a heavy breath said that he was too old to be using that much magic in go.

The other soldier grabbed Talia and the three ran. They could hear the sound of fighting in the stronghold behind them. Talia briefly looked back only to see smoke and fire raging all over the city and castle.

"We need to get her where there are more men." Oisin said to the other soldier.

The soldier said that the legion in Charwood was the closest to them. It was then the sound of a branch snapping to the side of the road made them stop. Oisin drew his sword as well as the soldier. Talia, having dropped her knife in the castle grabbed a rock from the road and wiped her eyes. It was then Captain Rollins emerged from the forest and was shocked to see Talia covered in blood with her clothes torn. Talia dropped the rock in her hand and ran to the captain, hugging him tightly.

"Mother is dead! Balor killed her!" she said falling to his waist.

Captain Rollins was shocked by the news and looked to Oisin and the soldier.

"What happened?" he asked with horror.

Oisin explained everything and said they were going to take her back to Charwood for her safety. Captain Rollins looked down at Talia and helped her up.

"Talia, look at me." He said checking to see if she was okay. "You are no longer safe here. You have to go somewhere they will not find you. I will go north and help find Lady Aine's crystal."

Talia grabbed Captain Rollins hand which rested on her shoulder and said she couldn't leave. Captain Rollins grabbed Talia's cheeks.

"YOU MUST! The only reason people have the will to fight for their freedom is because you and your family are a reminder that it is possible. If you die that hope will fade and the people will lose the will to fight. You must go!"

Oisin asked where they could take her. Captain Rollins thought and looked around, then the thought struck him.

"The human realm."

Oisin and the soldier were shocked by the captain's statement.

"Sir you can't be serious?" Oisin exclaimed.

Captain Rollins said that he was and looked to Talia.

"I just sent Samuel and his sister through the portal myself. You need to find them and hide until I come for you. Can you find your way to the portal from here?"

Talia sniffled and said that she could. Captain Rollins nodded and hugged her tightly. He then drew his sword and handed it to Talia, telling her to hurry and stay safe. Oisin asked what they were to do; Captain Rollins told them to escort Talia to the portal and he would head north immediately. With a final hug the captain let go of Talia and whistled. His horse came from out of the woods and he mounted it.

"Don't delay!" he shouted "Hurry to the portal!" with that Captain Rollins rode away at break neck speed.

The soldier looked down at Oisin and he looked back.

"I don't like this plan sir." the soldier said with worry.

Oisin agreed, but said that it was the only plan they had for now. The three hurried into the forest and up two hills before they reached the portal. They had walked for so long in the forest that the morning sun was now shining down upon them.

"The portal stone is here your Majesty." Oisin said peering through a bush.

The three broke through the thick undergrowth into the clearing where the stone was. The soldier ran over and immediately drew the Celtic knot upon its surface. The portal burst open with a gust of wind and light.

"Hurry your Majesty. It is open." The soldier said flagging her over.

As Talia and Oisin walked over the sound men on horseback coming up the hill on the dirt road frightened them. Oisin looked down the road and then to Talia "Go!" he shouted drawing his blade.

"We will divert them for now. Just Go!"

Talia was hesitant, but before she could do anything the soldier grabbed her and threw her into the portal. He then closed the portal behind her, leaving her only one way to go. Talia was safe for now and she had to find Samuel. She hoped that with his help they might be able to save the kingdom.

CHAPTER TEN

Upon hearing Talia's tale Samuel smashed his fist onto the table next to him.

"Had I been there I could have helped in some way." He said gritting his teeth.

Talia sat her cup down and looked to the ground. "Samuel, even if you had been there. There was no way for you or I to stand against Balor."

Magdalen sat with her hand over mouth and muttered that she could not believe that the Dark King had returned. Emily was confused as she did not know whom anyone in Talia's story was, but she could feel that the events she had described were grave in nature.

"How do we stop him then?" asked Samuel "How did your grandmother stop him?"

Talia fell back onto the chair she was sitting and placed both of her hands on her face.

"My grandmother had the help of Master Senan and Lady Aine and an army. We have nothing in those terms. I don't know if my father's armies still exist."

Samuel stood "If retired soldiers whom served your father were willing to still fight, I'm sure there are more out there. As for wizards or witches I'm not sure what we could do. You sent men as well as Captain Rollins to find Lady Aine's crystal. We can only hope they find it."

Talia dropped her arms and huffed "I just feel useless. For the first time since Tomlin was killed, I feel helpless in the events around me."

Magdalen leaned over to Talia and placed her hand on her knee.

"Your Majesty I can tell you one thing. When you get as old as I am you learn that things eventually work out. We may not see it in the moment and it may be a long time, but life always has a good end if we work hard towards it."

Magdalen's words seemed to touch Talia's heart and a small smile came upon her face. Samuel then placed his hand on Talia's shoulder and she looked up to him.

"I may be a human, but I will fight by your side. If it were not for you and your father Emily would not be standing here by my side again." Emily then walked over to Samuel's side and placed her hand on her brothers back.

"I am confused by many things that have happened and do not know how I may be able to help. But as Samuel said we owe a debt of gratitude to you and we must repay it."

As Emily said these words Talia had another tear fall from her eye. Samuel chuckled and a smile came over his face. He took the rag from before and wiped the tear from Talia's cheek.

"You are not alone."

Talia smiled and grabbed Samuel's hand.

"Master Senan was right. We did act like children before."

Samuel laughed and agreed with her. Magdalen stood and clapped her hands together.

"Well, we must wait for the captain to come get you in the meantime. They day is young and I have much to do. Clean, cook, go to market, get more wood for the fire. To top it all off I must prepare a room for your Majesty. Busy, busy, busy." Magdalen began to scramble around and clean up her home. Samuel laughed as he, Talia, and Emily watched.

"We must go and set our home in order as well. Talia if you wish to accompany us, we can get you some new clothes."

Emily then reminded Samuel that Talia would stand out in their world. "She is not of human birth Samuel. She will be spotted if we see anyone."

Talia took Samuel's hand from her shoulder and stood. She thought for a moment and remembered something that she had forgot. Reaching into her pocket Talia grabbed the stone that Master Senan had given her.

"With all that has happened I forgot about this." she said holding it up.

Samuel was surprised and thought aloud "I think I lost the one I had when I found Emily."

Emily scoffed in response "You always seem to misplace something brother."

Talia laughed and agreed with Emily "He has lost a few swords if I am not mistaken."

Samuel was at a loss for words and did not know how to respond. Emily walked over to the door of the small cottage and grabbed a cloche.

"Brother, we have a few days journey do we not? We must be going."

Samuel nodded to his sister and looked to Magdalen whom was now sweeping her floor.

"Will you be alright on your own for a few days?"

Magdalen laughed and waved her hand "Oh yes dear. I have been on my own before and no one wants anything to do with a one-hundred-year-old hermit in the woods."

Samuel was shocked by Magdalens age. "She moves very well to be that old." he thought with surprise. Talia smiled as she watched Magdalen scurry around.

"I heard stories of when she served my grandmother. They say that she had the energy of a dozen people and the work ethic of a thousand workers. It looks like that energy has not waned."

Talia then sighed and looked back to the stone in her hand. She took and placed it around her neck and a flash of light filled the room. Talia's ears became rounded and her skin became less vibrant as it was before. Talia now looked as a human. She looked over her hands and down at her body with amazement. She then looked up to Samuel and Emily and asked how she looked. Samuel was stunned for though Talia now looked human; she seemed to have an, other worldly beauty about her that he could see.

"Breath taking." was the only words that left Samuel's mouth.

Talia blushed at the compliment. Emily sighed and said that she still felt uncomfortable with them using magic.

"It's not right brother. We were always told that magic was only used by God or the Devil and if those on earth use it then only the Devil is at play."

Samuel turned to Emily and placed his hand on her shoulder.

"Emily they are not devils nor evil in any way. Talia has shown nothing but kindness to us. I owe her my life for the help she has given me in finding you."

Emily was still visibly uncomfortable with the thought and asked that she not be reminded of it. Samuel nodded and agreed to his sister's request.

"Well, we best be off if we are to have a few days journey to your home." Talia said grabbing the sword Captain Rollins had given her and placing it in her belt.

Emily walked over to Talia and said that she could not wear the sword and they would have to get her a dress when they went to market. Talia was stunned by Emily's words and asked why she would have to do these things. Samuel cleared his throat, but before he could explain Emily did it for him.

"Because women are not allowed to be soldiers or fighters in our world and must wear clothes that have been deemed proper."

Talia was surprised by this and looked to Samuel. Samuel rubbed the back of his neck and said that their world was different in its customs.

"But what difference does it make if I know how to handle a blade or that I prefer to wear trousers over a dress?" asked Talia.

Emily explained in detail that that is what the King of England, the Church of England had decreed.

"It's proper for a lady to look and act a lady." "I am still confused." Talia replied.

Samuel then said that it would draw less attention to her and give her better chance of staying hidden for now. Talia was not happy that she had to hide in such a manner. However, Samuel did indeed carry a point in agreeing with Emily. Less attraction would make her safer in this realm. The three thanked Magdalen for all her help and to keep her eyes open for any sign of Captain Rollins. Talia would return once she had gotten better clothing and rested.

"Be careful dears." Magdalen said as she hugged each of them.

The three then set off, heading for Samuel and Emily's family farm. As they traveled through the forest, Talia was not impressed with the human realm. It more or less seemed like her own realm save for the exclusion of magic beings. Upon reaching their home Samuel and Emily were shocked to find that the roof had been torn away and much of their farming tools gone.

"We must have been looted by people whom thought this place abandon." said Samuel as looked the home over. "It will take some work, but I should be able to craft a new roof with in a day or two. I had been meaning to do away with the straw roof and put a wooden shingle one on."

Emily dropped to her knees and hugged the ground. "Thank God above that I am home. I never thought I would see it again."

Talia helped Emily back to her feet and gave her comfort.

"Well..." Samuel said placing his hands on his hips "The day is not half done and we still need to get you new clothes and I need to get new tools and lumber."

Samuel then walked over to a stone wall that sat on the far edge of the farm. He looked for a rock in the wall and pulled a particularly dark one from the wall. With a sigh of relief Samuel shouted

"It is still here!"

He then took a wooden box from behind where the stone sat and opened it. With a nod he walked over to Emily and Talia and showed them what was inside.

"Father left us a small number of coins when he passed, and I have been adding a coin each week to it. We should have enough saved for what we need."

Talia looked and then pulled a small purse from her pocket.

"This is the last bit of gold I have upon my person from our journey."

Samuel took the bag and looked in "Talia, I am grateful for the jester, but I fear we cannot use your coins here. Your coins do not have the face of our King, King Charles the Second."

Talia nodded and put the bag back in her pocket. Samuel placed his hand on her arm and thanked her again.

"Keep your gold for when you return home."

Samuel then handed the box to Emily and asked her to hold it as he looked to see if their cart had been taken. Samuel then walked over to the small stone barn that sat adjacent to the home. As he opened the wooden barn doors, he found a small cart just big enough to haul tools and some goods. It would struggle to haul anything else though and Samuel realized this. With a sigh Samuel grabbed the dust and web covered cart and pulled it from the barn.

"I fear I may have to spend every coin just for us to have the lumber for a roof and a cart to haul it."

The three then set off for Dartmoor with some haste as to not lose what was left of the day. When they arrived Samuel and Emily found that the town had been repaired from the attack. Many people took notice of Emily and Samuel and stared. Some whispered amongst themselves as the three walked down the dirt streets. It was then the Sheriff saw them and ran up to them.

"Samuel! Emily! God above! You're alive?!" The Sheriff exclaimed with shock.

Samuel let go of his cart and wiped his hands upon his trousers.

"I told you I would find Emily and save her."

The Sheriff was surprised and could not help but smile.

"That you did boy, that you did." were the only words he could muster through his smile.

The Sheriff then looked to Talia and asked whom she was. Samuel stumbled slightly over his words, but Emily was quick to intervene.

"This is our cousin Talia. She is Welsh and has come to help us tend the farm for the last part of the season."

The Sheriff hummed and replied

"I did not know your family had Welsh in it. Well, we shall not hold that against you and that would explain why you are not properly dressed."

Talia was taken back by the Sheriffs brashness. Emily and Samuel laughed and said they had come for supplies for the farm and new clothes for Talia. The Sheriff nodded.

"Speaking of your farm I saw that the straw had been taken from its roof. I suppose that you had been gone so long that folks thought you wouldn't miss the roof gone. Before I go any further, I have to know Samuel, how did you save Emily from that beast?"

Samuel patted the Sheriff's shoulder "You, said I would think you mad when you told me what had happened. Now I say the same to you in regards to saving her."

The Sheriff huffed and his eyes widened.

"Indeed. The town council has agreed never to speak of what had happened. We all agreed that if anyone should ask how so many of our people died, we will say it was Typhoid. So, keep in mind not to bring it up. Some of the town's folk are still shaky and the bishop has warned not to speak of it. For "It may bring the devil back." Now enough idle chatter, Emily welcome back and I am glad you're both safe. Now go help your cousin get dressed properly before the bishop sees her. Samuel you and I should go see about getting you a new roof."

The Sheriff put his arm around Samuel's neck as they walked off. Emily looked up to Talia whom was looking all around at the shops and homes. "It's odd." said Talia "Your realm is near no different than mine and yet they are separate because of petty squabbles and prejudice."

Emily was unsure of how to respond and grabbed the cart.

"Come with me." she said pulling the cart passed Talia "The seamstress is this way."

Talia followed Emily down the narrow street which raised up a small incline hill. To the left of the street was a small open space which men were laying the ground work for a new building. To the right were several houses of wood and stone, with a single wooden post that had a hook and lantern upon it. At the top of the inclined street on the right was the seamstress shop. A large wooden sign with a ball of string and needle painted upon it, hung low from a black iron hook. Emily let go of the cart and left it on the edge of the street. The two then walked into the shop to find and old woman about in her sixties and a young woman in her thirties sewing a blanket. The old woman, whom was hunched from years of looking down to sew looked up and gasped.

"I saw you taken by the devil a few months ago? How are you here?" she asked holding her hand to her mouth.

Emily replied that she had been saved by her brother and that God was good enough to deliver her from evil. The old woman lowered her hand and shook her head

"Dear oh dear. I pray that evil has not touched they soul child."

The old woman then looked to Talia

"Child what are you doing wearing trousers and your blouse is in such a state."

Emily told the old woman that that was the reason for their visit, to acquire a new outfit for her. The old woman looked to the younger across from her and asked her to go in the back with the Talia and get her into more suitable clothing. The younger girl made a final stitch on the blanket and tied it. She then cut the string and threw the blanket off and stood. The girl asked Talia to follow her in the back of the shop behind a wooden door. Talia looked to Emily and Emily gave her assurance that everything would be well. Talia looked back to the woman and followed her through the door into a small room with a table and a small window up high for light. In the room was a standing wardrobe of ash and the woman opened it.

Inside the wardrobe were serval shirts, trousers, and dresses of different shapes, sizes, and colors. The woman took a dark green dress and held it up to Talia saying that it would be lovely on her. The woman then grabbed a cream color blouse and handed it to her as well. Talia looked at the green dress and took note of a lacing around the top of the breast. The woman then handed her a white shawl with small knotted tassels hanging from it. Then she pulled a bonnet of white out to match it. Talia asked if all of the layers of clothing where necessary. The woman replied.

"Yes, it is. A woman should be dressed proper and decent. Show modesty in this world."

The woman then stepped out of the room and told Talia to come out when she is finished. Talia looked over the clothes as the woman shut the door.

"If it would not raise attention, I would not wear such regalia." she muttered to herself.

Talia put the clothes on, and immediately hated it. She did not like how the dress constrained her movement or how it went to the ground. Talia stepped out putting the bonnet upon her head.

Emily and the two women looked at Talia as she stepped out of the room. The younger woman walked over and checked the fit on Talia, asking her how it felt. Talia replied with a huff.

"It's a bit constraining."

The older woman scoffed at the comment.

"You children today have more freedom in your attire then I did in my day."

The younger woman pulled on the dress and said that it was good fit for Talia. Emily pulled out four silver coins from a small purse attached to her belt and handed it to the older woman.

"Thank you for the new clothing." she said putting the leather strap back on her purse.

The old woman looked at the coins with her boney finger.

"Dear I owe you a quarter. Give me a moment."

The old woman then handed the coin to the younger and the woman took the coin to a nearby table. She then took a small hammer and a metal cutter and struck the coin cutting it in four. The woman then handed a piece back to Emily and thanked them for their business. Talia and Emily then stepped out back onto the street. Emily asked if Talia felt okay in her new clothes.

"I don't like how they restrict my movement. Why did they cut the coin in four?"

Emily paused at Talia's question and explained that that was how change was made. Talia cocked her brow and said that it was odd and seemed to waist coins. Emily once again was unsure of how to respond. These customs were every day occurrences to her, but to Talia they were foreign and strange. Samuel came up to the two about that time, behind him was a flat cart with boards stacked and strapped upon it.

"Thankfully I had enough to get everything for our new roof, but I fear we are now broke." He said huffing while pulling the cart.

Emily looked in her purse and said that she had only a coin and a quarter left after buying Talia's new clothes. Samuel looked over Talia and was stunned by her new look.

"It fits you well." He said setting the cart down.

Talia looked down and said that she felt strange wearing such clothes. Samuel cleared his throat and suggested that they should be heading back home as the sun was soon to set. The three left Dartmoor and made their way back to the small farm. The sun had set near an hour ago and they had to travel by moonlight the last couple miles. Samuel and Emily set the two carts down outside the front door of the small home.

"Emily, why don't you go and light a fire inside. It may not get very warm for us, but at least we will have light."

Talia sat down on the edge of the cart with the boards and looked up to the star filled sky as Emily went into the home.

"It reminds me of when we traveled to Master Senan's. You were right Samuel; the night sky here is just as beautiful as it was back in my land." she said trying to adjust the dress.

Samuel walked over to Talia and sat down next to her.

"If only we knew everything that was to happen from that point. Maybe we could have done something different." he said as he sat.

Talia nodded

"And maybe then I would not be in this accursedly fitting dress and.... mother

and father would still be alive. I hope that Captain Rollins can find the crystal. I saw the power that Balor had and I see why it took both Master Senan and Lasy Aine to defeat him."

It was then another tear fell from Talia's eye as she turned her gaze back to the stars. Samuel looked at her and rubbed his stubble covered chin.

"Talia" Samuel said with a slight pause "I wish I could undo all that has happened. Had it not been for me asking for your help, both your mother and father would still be alive."

Talia shook her head and told Samuel that everything had been planned before he ever came into her life.

"I think all this would have happened even had you and I not met. They had captured the Banshee. They prolonged my father's life only to take it when they deemed fit. Maybe this all happened sooner than it was supposed to, but it happened."

Samuel sighed through his nose and looked briefly to the ground, then up at the night sky. Talia then followed

"Honestly, I think one of the few good things that has happened during this was that I did meet you."

Samuel was taken back by Talia's words and looked at her. Talia looked down from the sky at Samuel and smiled.

"Even though you are human and I have been raised to believe your kind is dangerous and greedy. You have showed more kindness to me then I have you. Thank you."

Samuel was speechless. He did not know how to respond to Talia or her kind words. Talia then placed her hand on Samuel's cheek and leaned over to him. She kissed Samuel on the lips and then placed her forehead against his.

"Thank you." She said again letting go of his head and standing up.

Samuel was shaken and did not know how to reply or feel in the moment. Talia walked over to the door of the home and opened it. The light of a fire from inside illuminated the front half of Talia as she stood in the doorway.

Talia looked back to Samuel as he stood from the cart holding his bottom lip. Samuel looked up to Talia to find her smiling at him. She then let out a slight laugh and stepped into the house.

Samuel shook his head as he had never been kissed before. He then entered his home to find Emily pocking the fire and Talia sitting down on a small chair. Samuel looked at Talia to see her looking back at him. The night sky hung over their heads in the roofless home. Tomorow would bring many changes in all of their lives. For this is only one of the Legends of Dreegahnna.

To be continued in Legends of
Dreegahnna Volume: Two